Once Upon a Timepiece

STARR WOOD

Bo Tree Books

Published by Bo Tree Books 2013

Copyright © Starr Wood 2012

Starr Wood has asserted his right under the Copyright, Designs and Patents Act 1988 to be identified as the author of this work.

All rights reserved. No part of this publication may be reproduced, stored in a retrieval system, or transmitted, in any form or by any means, electronic, mechanical, photocopying, recording or otherwise, without the prior permission of the publishers.

This book is sold subject to the condition that it shall not, by way of trade or otherwise, be lent, resold, hired out, or otherwise circulated without the publisher's prior consent in any form of binding or cover other than that in which it is published and without a similar condition, including this condition, being imposed on the subsequent purchaser.

This is a work of fiction. The names, characters, locations and events are the product of the author's imagination or are used fictitiously. Any resemblance to persons, alive or dead, events or places is entirely coincidental.

First published in 2013 by Bo Tree Books

www.botreebooks.com

ISBN: 9780992770204

STARR WOOD

Starr Wood is a British journalist, writer and economist. He was born in England in 1970, but grew up in Nigeria, Ras Al Khaimah, South Korea, the Philippines, and Taiwan. In 1992, Starr graduated from the London School of Economics and began his career as a journalist working for a variety of news media in London and the Middle East. Since 1999, he has worked at The Economist Group, first in London, and then in Asia. Today, he lives in Singapore with his wife and three children. *Once Upon a Timepiece* is his debut novel.

www.onceuponatimepiece.com

For WW, MM, TM, and DC

1	January: Seize the day	9
2	February: The past is a foreign country	22
3	March: Moment of truth	34
4	April: Time is money	51
5	May: Time flies	62
6	June: The reunion	75
7	July: Doing time	90
8	August: A time of pharaohs	101
9	September: To everything there is a season	126
10	October: History repeats itself	138
11	November: Better never than late	152
12	December: Memory lane	166

1

JANUARY: SEIZE THE DAY

Conrad Sands slipped off his watch and placed it on the desk in front of him. He stared at the second-hand ticking neatly, inevitably, dispassionately round the face, measuring out increments of life with blank indifference. How many seconds had passed since he had last seen her?

Conrad pulled a sheet of paper towards him and began to scribble dates and numbers. He worked absently, only half-engaged with the task. June 22nd 1992 he wrote at the top. That was the last time he had seen Mariana Carson. He couldn't remember the exact time. Perhaps it was 8.30am when she had climbed into a London cab with her bags and sped off to Victoria station, and then to Gatwick for her flight to New York.

He had stayed with her that last night in her rented apartment above a newsagents on Wardour Street in Soho. They had risen early and walked round to the Patisserie Valerie café on Old Compton Street just as it was opening. It was her favourite place for breakfast—always pain au chocolat and a caffe latte, sitting at an outside table, watching the day come to life. The street had a grubby cheerfulness, the gutters full of beer cans and cigarette butts from the night before that would be cleared away by roadsweepers as the crisp morning air brightened with the sun.

Today was January 12th, 2012. Nineteen and a half years had passed since that morning—7,143 days. Conrad put down his pencil. It was a quarter of a lifetime.

He had only known her for nine months, and yet the memories he had of her were as clear today as they were in the moments after she had slipped away in her taxi that summer morning. At least they felt just as clear.

He pulled open the desk drawer and took out a second watch, cleaning it on his shirt. He had never worn this one, but he had held it countless times over the past 19 years, staring at its features. The watch was a 1946 Breitling Chronomat made from rose-coloured gold. Mariana had told him it was designed during World War II for aviators. It had two extra dials on its face and a rotating bezel marked with various scales and measurements. In the right hands, the watch could be used to work out speeds, distances, percentages, fuel consumption and numerous other calculations.

Mariana had given him the watch over their last breakfast. It had belonged to her grandfather, who had left it to her in his will. Mariana had worn it every day that Conrad had known her. It was one of his defining memories of her—a slim 23-year-old woman wearing an antique men's gold watch that dwarfed her wrist. The leather strap showed clearly where she had punched an extra hole to make the fit tight enough.

Conrad had protested at the gift, but Mariana had waved away his concerns and insisted he keep it to remind him of her. At the time it had felt like a promise to keep in close contact, that their parting was just a temporary break. He had been 21, and thought they'd be apart for a few months, perhaps a year at most. He certainly hadn't expected to be 40 years old when they reconnected.

He wound up the Breitling and set the time so that it now ticked in unison with his first watch. It was 5.30pm, and already dark outside. He was due to meet her in two hours.

Conrad showered and shaved and stared at his reflection through the bathroom steam. At 21 he'd been athletic, choosing to cycle whenever he travelled across London. He had been a keen windsurfer at home in his native Cornwall, and was a regular in a five-a-side soccer league. Now the mirror showed a man in much poorer shape. These days he jogged to keep fit, but it hadn't prevented his paunch from filling out and his skin from losing its elasticity. His hair was still thick and dark, but his face seemed more bloated.

How would Mariana have aged? At 23 she had been striking, if not classically beautiful. She had given Conrad the strong impression of a native American Indian, a hunter—slim, with sinuous limbs, long black hair and olive skin. She caught people's eye and held it, but it wasn't so much prettiness or good looks as it was an impression of something exotic, a determination, a confidence. She saw the world in her own way, and meeting her made you want to understand how and why.

He had first met her in the student bar at the London School of Economics. It was the winter term of his final year. He was playing pool with a friend when she'd challenged him to a game. She lost the first, but challenged him again and again, until she beat him on the fourth try. Conrad was a good player who rarely lost. He maintained that he'd let her win out of pity, but it wasn't true.

Mariana, whose swarthy complexion was a blend of Venezuelan mother and Anglo Saxon father, was an American exchange student from Duke University studying economics at the LSE for a year. She shared several classes with Conrad, and after that first encounter over the pool table they had spent more and more time together.

She was endlessly curious about London and its history, taking Conrad to museums, art galleries, churches and buildings that he had never seen. One of her more unusual interests centred on the graves of the famous. At Westminster Abbey she sought out the resting places of Alfred Tennyson, Charles Dickens, Isaac Newton and Charles Darwin. At St

Paul's Cathedral, she visited the graves of John Donne, Alexander Fleming, William Blake and Christopher Wren.

Once, Conrad had taken her to see a football match, a Chelsea game at Stamford Bridge. She had loved the gruff cynicism of the life-long supporters as they watched the match, and afterwards they had drunk in a local pub called the Pickled Pelican with a boisterous crowd of fans. Mariana liked to drink—Jim Beam bourbon and beer. On leaving the pub, she had taken Conrad to Brompton Cemetery next to the football ground to seek out the grave of Emmeline Pankhurst, the suffragette. It had taken them some time to find it, and when they did, Mariana had sat on the ground and smoked a cigarette, suddenly quiet, the rowdiness of the stadium and the pub lost to personal contemplation.

On another occasion, a Saturday morning, Mariana had announced that she was going to Highgate Cemetery to see the grave of Karl Marx. The great European experiment with communism had collapsed in the previous two years and she wanted to see where its architect lay. They had stood together in front of the austere cuboid of grey granite, topped by a giant bust of the man, and talked about Marx's theories, his delusions and his legacy.

As an economics student, Conrad was familiar with Marx and had denounced his ideology. So too had Mariana, but her arguments had seemed so much more passionate and nuanced, so much more intense than Conrad's text-book clichés.

Conrad knew that she was well-read. Her father, an engineer who ran a company in New York that made electricity transmission machinery, had banned television from his household. He believed in the merits of discussion, debate, reading and study. Conrad had found it somewhat ironic that a man who spent his life improving the delivery of electricity to people's homes, should forbid the watching of television in his own, but Mariana had clearly benefitted from his discipline.

In one or two instances, Conrad had found himself reading ahead so as to impress Mariana with his own erudition. When she made plans to visit Kensal Green Cemetery, and the graves of Charles Babbage, the mathematician, and Anthony Trollope—"an economist's novelist", as Mariana described him—Conrad spent a week reading and improving his knowledge of both of them.

Conrad hadn't thought to ask her why she was so keen to see these graves. Looking back, he supposed it was to bring the figures of history to life for her in some way. She seemed to admire great achievement. She seemed to hold great respect for men and women who had used their "brief candle", their "hour upon the stage" as Macbeth put it, to make a difference.

Conrad flipped the Breitling watch over and looked at the back where an inscription read "May your brief candle shine brightly". Conrad had only seen the inscription after she had given him the watch. No doubt it had been engraved by her grandfather, or by whoever had given it to him. But Conrad had often wondered over the past nineteen years if the dictum had held a special resonance for Mariana. The inscription was part advocacy, urging the wearer to live life fully, and part prayer. Perhaps it was a sense of life's brevity that had so animated Mariana's interest in the graves of London's great achievers.

It certainly seemed that Mariana's candle had shone brightly. In the past few weeks Conrad had learned a little about her life since they'd parted. Her year studying at LSE was the last of her undergraduate degree, and before she left London she had secured a place at Harvard to study for a masters degree in law. That much Conrad had always known. He had tried to stay in touch, writing letters to her family address in New York. He wrote six times in the first eight months but never heard back from her. He had no idea if the address had been wrong or if she had simply lost interest in him.

Those were the days when the web was still in its infancy and keeping in touch with distant friends was hard. As the internet blossomed, however, Conrad had come across traces of Mariana and the work she was doing. An online search on her name in 1998 showed that she was working in Bosnia, helping to re-establish property rights for families displaced by the Yugoslavia conflict.

Three years later, in 2001, another search revealed that she had set up an organisation called Rule of Law— its motto was "Nobody above the law, nobody below the law". Its website described a group of lawyers fighting for the formalisation of property rights in the world's squatter settlements and conflict zones. The philosophy behind the group was exactly what Conrad would have expected from Mariana: clear deeds and ownership rights to land were the foundation of wealth. Without formal property rights, the poor had no assets against which to borrow, they were unable to set up or to own legally-recognised businesses, and they were excluded from the formal economy. Only by establishing property rights for the poor could they improve their lives. Marx would be turning in his grave, Conrad had thought on reading it.

As the years had gone by, Conrad's thoughts had turned to Mariana less and less frequently, but her presence still lingered at the edge of his consciousness. Every few months he would trawl the web to see what new mentions he could find of her. Disappointingly, he had never found any photographs. She wasn't registered with any of the social media sites, and although she was quoted periodically in news stories, they never carried a picture.

At various times he had composed emails to Mariana— some of them long and heartfelt, others short and pithy—but he had never sent them. He had always arrived at the same conclusion, that Mariana had forgotten about him and moved on. Why else had she ignored his letters? He had given her his family's address in Cornwall before she'd left London. She could easily have written to him, but she never did.

Over the years, Conrad's impression of his nine-month relationship with her had grown gradually less certain. Had he simply been a friend of convenience, an easy companion in a foreign city? Perhaps he had been even less than that. Certainly it was she who had initiated the friendship, but was it he who had sustained it? Had Mariana invited him to accompany her on her explorations of London, or had he invited himself?

Throughout their time together it was a frustration for Conrad that they never had sex, not once. It wasn't through any sense of prudence or chastity on her part. Mariana had been happy to kiss him, and to share a bath with him as they smoked joints and drank wine and listened to The Grateful Dead and Neil Young and Funkadelic. She had been happy to sleep in the same bed as him, both of them naked, caressing each other and talking. But anything more and she had gently declined.

The reason she gave for her restraint was the ending of a long relationship just before she came to London. Mariana had said she wasn't ready to step straight into a new one, and Conrad had believed her. But in the years since, he had wondered whether the previous boyfriend had really existed. He had also considered the possibility that this boyfriend had been all too real and waiting for her in New York or at Duke. Conrad imagined him as tall and tanned, an impressive man with great charisma.

But if all that were true, then why had she given him the watch? Surely such a treasured heirloom handed down from her grandfather wouldn't be so easily lost to a passing fling of no significance? If only they had made love. Somewhere deep inside himself, Conrad suspected that some of his enduring interest in Mariana was thanks to the unrequited nature of his love for her.

Conrad padded through into his bedroom. It was still littered with boxes and packing cases that had arrived a few days earlier. He'd spent the past fifteen years in Asia, working in Tokyo, Singapore and Hong Kong, before deciding to return to the UK. He'd sold most of his possessions before the move. All that remained were a handful of books, two paintings, an antique chest from Nepal, his golf clubs, and several cartons of photographs and papers. At the time, Conrad had thought it a good idea to get rid of all the clutter in his life, but surveying the items that had survived his cull, it didn't seem like much.

He shrugged to himself and began to get dressed. He could always buy more things if he wanted to. A career spent working as a fund manager meant he was already wealthy. He didn't have a job in London, but nor did he need one. His return to the UK was a chance for him to reassess his life and decide what he wanted to do next. He needed a change of scene.

For some time, he'd felt a growing disillusionment gnawing at his soul. Partly it was a sense that his job, indeed his whole industry, had lost its way. It no longer provided social utility. But more than that, Conrad was consumed with a gathering sense that he wasn't the person he thought he'd be at the age of 40. He hadn't lived the life he'd wanted to live, and time was getting shorter.

Occasionally he'd hear a piece of music and be transported back twenty years to a different era, to a different version of himself, a younger version, a better version. It might be Lou Reed's "Sweet Jane" or Blue Cheer's "The Pilot" or any number of other songs. More and more, these tunes took him back to a place that increasingly looked nothing like his life today. They unlocked a time of possibility, a place without borders, a world of potential and greatness and passion. It wasn't only music, it was also books and art and conversations. More and more they filled him with a sense of a past vision for his life, a hope, an expectation that he had failed to achieve. Conrad was filled with a sense that, if his younger self could see him now, he would have been disappointed.

On returning to London six weeks earlier, Conrad had contacted many of the friends he'd lost touch with over the years. He had emailed Mariana too, spending a long time crafting his message, trying to get the tone right. He wanted to appear friendly but casual, interested but not overly so. He avoided any mention of his unanswered letters, or questions of why she had never been in touch. He was just an old friend re-establishing contact.

She had replied almost immediately, her email full of

enthusiasm and delight at hearing from him. She said she'd missed him and wanted to know what he'd been up to in the years since university. Her response made Conrad feel ashamed that he had pretended to be so blasé, and so they had emailed back and forth, filling in the history that each of them had missed.

Mariana was still unmarried, and still lived in New York, although she spent most of her life on the road, meeting the donors who funded her organisation, recruiting lawyers to join it, and leading efforts to represent the poor and displaced in their legal disputes. Much of her time was spent in Venezuela, Colombia, Ecuador, Guyana and Suriname. She described her work as frustrating and rewarding in equal measure. Occasionally it was dangerous too.

Mariana told how she had come to truly understand the importance of land rights in the months between leaving LSE and attending Harvard. She had been visiting her mother's family in Caracas in Venezuela and had witnessed first-hand a riot in one of the barrios in the hills rising out of the city. She had travelled to the barrio alone, wanting to understand the plight of the urban poor, and had become caught up in an outbreak of violence that had put her in hospital.

She had spent the next five months recovering from her injuries—a slow, painful and frustrating experience that had delayed her start at Harvard. But the experience was an epiphany, it had changed her life. She had witnessed the desperate anger of people trying to protect the pitiful plots that they and their families had worked for, but which the law said they didn't own.

Conrad had still not spoken to Mariana. All their communication had been via email, and it seemed better that way. It had allowed him the space to grow comfortable with her once more. Tonight, however, they would meet face-to-face for the first time in nineteen and a half years. One week earlier, Mariana had emailed saying that she was coming to London for four days. She was meeting several law firms that wanted to get involved with her cause. She wondered if she could see him too?

Conrad strapped the Breitling onto his wrist and checked the time—one hour to go. It seemed right to wear the watch tonight. It would show how important she had remained to him, and that he had never stopped thinking about her. He didn't know what to expect from the evening. The two of them were both single. Possibly it would lead to a rekindling of the past. Perhaps he had held a place in Mariana's heart for the past nineteen years, just as she had in his. He felt calm as he set off to meet her.

The venue for their reunion was a wine bar in Notting Hill called Wild Thyme, just off the Portobello Road. It served tapas-style food and was a suitably casual place for the occasion. On a Thursday night it would be busy but comfortable.

As Conrad approached, he stopped outside to peer through the plate-glass windows. The lights inside were dimmed, but thick church candles flickered from sconces on the walls and from tall wooden candlesticks. It looked warm against the icy darkness of the street. Many of the tables had people sitting at them.

Conrad stepped inside and surveyed the room, looking for her. The space was large and irregular, and parts of it were obscured by columns and corners. Mariana wasn't in the front part of the bar, and Conrad moved further in to get a better view of the back. And then he saw her. She was at the bar alone, sitting on a bar stool, straight-backed, with a glass of red wine in front of her. She looked poised and comfortable, and Conrad watched as she sipped her wine and tapped at her phone.

She was wearing jeans tucked into knee-length boots and a tight-fitting grey jumper. On the stool next to her lay a black overcoat. If anything, she looked more imposing than Conrad remembered. Her face was noticeably older, but her hair was still long and black and her figure still slender. Her expression was immediately familiar, but had gained a wisdom that Conrad realised had been inevitable. Her confidence at 23 had matured into a powerful presence.

"Can I find you a table, Sir?" A waiter said, approaching Conrad.

"No, no," he stammered, ducking behind a pillar. "Thank you, I'll sit at the bar. I'm meeting somebody."

"Can I take your coat?"

"In a minute, thank you."

His calmness had given way to trepidation. There she was, Mariana Carson, the woman who had lit up his life so brightly nineteen years earlier, and whose memory had stayed with him so persistently ever since. Conrad peered round the pillar again and was struck with familiar impressions: a hunter, a fierce intellect, an exotic beauty, a deep passion and energy and curiosity for life. But now he saw something else too, a sense of accomplishment that magnified all her earlier traits. She had grown in stature.

The more Conrad looked, the more his desire to meet Mariana drained away. She had achieved so much of value with her life. She had done such important work. Conrad felt thin and insignificant. Hers had been a life that deserved a grave worth visiting. Would anyone visit his in the years ahead?

Conrad called over the waiter, borrowed his pen and tore a page off his order pad. He leant against the pillar and wrote a note onto the page, before folding it in half. He unbuckled the Breitling watch, and cleaned it for the last time on his shirt, watching how the flickering candle flames on the wall above him reflected off the glass.

He stole one more glance at Mariana, and then gave the note and watch to the waiter and instructed him to give them to the woman at the bar. He made sure the waiter had understood the instructions clearly, and then pulled open the door and strode away into the cold.

"Where is he?" the woman asked when the waiter handed over the watch.

"He left. You might still catch him if you run."

She opened the folded note. It read:

Mariana—I saw you this evening sitting at the bar and you looked magnificent. You have become the woman I always imagined you'd be. I wanted to join you, with all my heart I wanted to, but I think too much time has passed. Or perhaps not enough time. I'm returning your grandfather's watch. You deserve it more than me. Conrad

"Do you want me to see if I can catch him?" the waiter asked.

"No… no thank you," the woman shook her head. "It's fine."

She read the note several more times and studied the watch, turning it over and reading the inscription on the back. She sipped her wine slowly, casting her eyes over the rest of the room, and when her glass was empty she asked the barman for her bill. A leather bag lay on the floor next to her barstool and she picked it up, dropping the letter and watch into it and pulling out her purse. She paid the bill and was putting on her coat when another woman joined her at the bar.

"Has there been a man in here looking for someone? Looking for a woman? He's about 40, tallish, dark hair," the second woman asked the barman. He shook his head. "If anyone does ask, maybe you could point him in my direction. I'm sitting in the corner over there."

"Sure," the barman said. "What's your name?"

"Mariana. And his name is Conrad. I'm worried he might have been in and missed me."

On hearing the conversation, the first woman turned and stared at Mariana. She had a face that wasn't easy to look at. Beneath her greying hair, her right cheek and temple looked as if they had been scalded by boiling water. While one side of her face had smooth skin the other side looked stretched and distorted like melted plastic.

"Has someone stood you up?" the first woman asked.

"I hope not," Mariana replied. "Hopefully he's just late. He's an old friend."

"Bloody men. I'm sure he'll show up." The first woman smiled, picked up her bag and walked out.

2

FEBRUARY: THE PAST IS A FOREIGN COUNTRY

Abigail Winter opened the cupboard in the hallway of her parents' house in Wandsworth and shuddered. It was piled high with boxes and old shoes and coats that hadn't been worn for years. The smell of mould and mothballs was both familiar and repellent, just like all the other smells in the house. The masculine perfume of her father's tin of shaving powder in the bathroom. The antiseptic odour of her mother's pantry. The cloying air-freshener in the living room.

They were smells from a different era, from a distant childhood—everything in the house was. The cut-glass ashtrays that sat unused on crochet tablecloths, the porcelain figurines of ballet dancers and society ladies on the mantelpiece, the silver-backed hairbrush on her mother's dressing table. What Abigail disliked most of all was the grandfather clock in the hall and the deep monotonous rhythm of its pendulum. To her ears it was the sound of death, a musty drum beat calling the elderly to their graves.

She pulled her father's coat from the cupboard, and James Winter stood patiently as his daughter wrapped him up. His scarf was too short to go round his neck twice and still have enough left over to tuck into his coat, but Abigail was determined.

"You're choking me," he protested.

"Nonsense," Abigail continued, twisting the scarf ever tighter. "It's freezing outside."

"Listen to her," Abigail's mother called from the kitchen behind the hall. "You don't want to catch what I've got."

"She's garrotting me."

"Do shut up, Dad. Here, take your hat and gloves." Abigail put on her own coat and moved to the front door. "Let's go, the cab's waiting."

She stepped out into the terraced street and walked to the curb. The street lamps were ringed with halos of misty yellow, their light barely reaching the squat brick houses that lined the road. Abigail liked it that way. During the day, it was all too easy to see the street's peeling paint and rubbish bins, the grimy windows and untended gardens full of weeds and cracked paving stones.

Abigail opened the door of the taxi and winced as her father laboured to climb in. If only her mother had been feeling better, she thought. She deserved a night out. She deserved to be treated to an occasion. It must be miserable for her living in that depressing street every day, with its run-down mediocrity measured out by the steady chimes of her clock. At least her father was coming. She could show him a good time, she could show him another side to life.

"We're going to a restaurant called L'Oeuf," Abigail said once they were in their seats.

"Lerf?" the driver asked.

"It's on Queen's Gate Mews. L'Oeuf, spelt L, O, E, U…"

"Yup, I know it," the driver interrupted. "Spanish is it?"

"French. It means 'egg'."

"An egg restaurant?" the driver said as he pulled away.

"They serve other food too. That's just the name," Abigail looked at her father and rolled her eyes.

"Have you got the letter?" her father asked. "You should

show it to them when we arrive, just so they know."

"I don't think I will," Abigail fished in her bag to find the letter and then tucked it back. "We'll get better service if they don't know."

"Why?"

"If I show it to them they'll think we can't afford to eat there. They'll treat us like second-class citizens."

"If you say so dear."

"It really ought to be Mum coming with you. I wish she'd been feeling better."

"She's very disappointed," her father nodded, "anyway, it's your letter. The meal was really meant for you."

"I eat in nice restaurants all the time."

"You said you'd never been there?"

"Not this one, but London has lots of good restaurants."

"Well, it's kind of you to think of us."

"Thank Avalon Capital," Abigail shrugged. "They're the ones who organised the raffle."

"I thought it was a Christmas present?"

"It was a raffle prize, at Avalon's Christmas party."

"What's his name, your boyfriend at Avalon?"

"Former boyfriend, Dad. His name's Philip. Complete wanker."

"Abi, please…"

"Well he was," Abigail pulled a compact from her bag and checked her face in its mirror. "At least we're getting a nice meal out of him," she flashed a forced smile at her father and clicked her compact shut. "We'll have to make sure we order the most expensive things on the menu."

The taxi sped across Wandsworth Bridge over the Thames and into Fulham. The dark terraced streets gave way to pubs and restaurants that spilled light onto the pavements where people huddled in groups filling the air with steam and cigarette smoke. They passed antiques shops full of Victorian chairs and Edwardian writing desks and elaborate model yachts. And as they drove closer to South Kensington, the houses grew taller and more imposing. With each passing kilometre Abigail felt her mood lift.

"Did you think about what I said? About you and Mum moving?" she asked.

"Don't go on about it dear," her father sighed. "We're quite happy where we are."

"None of your friends live there anymore."

"Some do…"

"And I don't like you and Mum walking those streets at night…" her mobile phone rang and Abigail pulled it out of her bag. "Sorry, it's work," she grimaced, "I won't be long."

Her father turned and looked through the window. They had reached Cromwell Road and the impressive architecture of the Natural History Museum. As a retired history teacher, he had herded countless groups of children, including Abigail, through its arched entrance on school trips. Seeing the building brought back memories that made him feel warm. He'd taught at the local school near his house. He'd spent his whole life there. He understood why his daughter wanted him to leave Wandsworth. She had moved up in the world. She worked as the office manager for a Swiss private bank. She spent her time with wealthy bankers and their even wealthier clients. But that wasn't his world.

"Here we are," the taxi driver said as he pulled over to the curb. James Winter peered through the window at the row of whitewashed Georgian houses with their columned entranceways and black railings. The restaurant was in a basement and marked by an awning of dark green fabric stretched over brass poles that covered the stairs down from the road. The name of the restaurant was printed in elaborate gold italics on the front of the awning.

"Here," Abigail said, handing her father a twenty-pound note. "Could you pay? I won't be a minute."

He did as he was asked and the two of them climbed out of the taxi and walked down the stairs to the restaurant. Inside, the hallway was warm and welcoming, with striped wallpaper, gilded paintings and a carpet of deep crimson. A man in his early thirties, dressed in a dinner jacket and with slicked-back hair, rushed out from behind a counter to greet them.

"Good evening sir, madam," he bowed slightly, the accent was foreign. "We are full this evening. I trust you have a reservation?"

"Yes," Abigail said, ending her call.

"Good, may I take your coats?" He helped Abigail and her father writhe free and hung the coats in a cupboard behind his desk.

"And the name?"

"It's Winter, Abigail Winter. We have a reservation for two at eight o'clock."

The man opened a large leather book and ran his finger down the page. A frown crossed his face. He flicked the page over, flicked it back and then looked at the preceding one.

"Could you spell it for me?"

"Winter?" Abigail looked bemused. "Just like the season."

"I'm afraid we don't have any record, madam. You're sure you made a reservation?"

"Yes, quite sure. I booked it three weeks ago. And I confirmed it on the phone this afternoon."

"I'm very sorry, madam, but your name isn't here. Perhaps you booked for another date?"

"No, it was for today. It must be in there. Look again. Winter, Abigail Winter, a table for two at 8.00pm."

"Please wait for a moment, madam," the man scurried off round the corner.

"Incompetence," Abigail muttered, drumming her fingers against the counter-top. "You'd expect better service than this wouldn't you?"

"I like their paintings," her father said, studying one in particular.

A moment later the man returned with his manager, also in a dinner jacket but much older. He was tall and wiry, with thinning black hair.

"Good evening," the second said. "I am Dmitri, the maitre d'hôtel. Can I help you?"

"I hope so," Abigail rounded on him. "I booked a table

for my father and I for 8.00pm this evening and you seem to have lost the reservation."

"Abigail Winter is the name?" He flicked through the leather book like the first had, turning pages back and forth. "I'm sorry madam, but we don't have you in here."

"Well could you put us in please?"

Dmitri closed the book and straightened to face Abigail. "Madam, I'm afraid we're full this evening. All the tables are booked."

"I hardly think that's my fault," Abigail's voice grew louder. "I called you three weeks ago to make a reservation. And I called again today, and whoever I spoke to, possibly you," she pointed to the first man who stood behind Dmitri, "told me everything was fine. This has been in our diaries for weeks. So please find us a table."

"But madam, as I said, all the tables are booked."

"And just as I said, that's not my fault."

"I appreciate what you're saying but…"

"Please don't try to 'manage' me with that conciliatory tone…"

Dmitri continued, "I assure you, madam, my staff and I never make mistakes with our bookings. There must be some sort of mix-up here."

"Bloody right there's been a mix-up."

"On any other day of the week we might have found you a spare table, but today is Friday, our busiest evening."

"I don't care what day it is…"

"Perhaps we could make a reservation for you next week? If you would like another Friday, then two weeks from now would be possible?"

"No," Abigail's voice rose still louder. "And I don't like your insinuation that I'm trying to bluff my way in. I called you twice and the reservation was clearly in your book."

"Madam, please keep your voice down, we have other diners…"

"Bloody lucky for them. You didn't screw up their reservations." Abigail paced back and forth. "I always thought of this place as being highly respected, but I can see I was misinformed."

"I'm sorry that you feel disappointed, madam, but…"

"You said your name was Dmitri?" Abigail asked. "What is that? Greek?"

"Yes, I am from Greece."

"Why doesn't that surprise me?"

"Madam?"

"The most shambolic country in Europe. Full of tax-dodgers and spongers, lying about their bloody finances, expecting everyone else to bail them out. It's no wonder this place is so disorganised."

"Abi dear, calm down," her father put his hand on her shoulder. "It doesn't matter. We can eat somewhere else."

"Of course it matters. I want to eat here."

"Why don't you show him the letter?"

She reached into her bag, opened the letter and tossed it onto the counter.

"Here," she said, pointing at the sheet of paper, "read that." Dmitri picked it up and read the letter slowly, then read it again.

"Is that current?" Abigail demanded. Dmitri read it once more and nodded slowly.

"It does seem to be madam."

"Of course it bloody is. And from a very serious company that spends a lot of money entertaining clients in places like this. So please find us a table."

"If you had shown me this letter sooner, madam, we could have avoided this situation. As it is…." Dmitri's voice trailed off. "If you'll excuse me, I'll see what I can do." He disappeared back round the corner, leaving the first man to stand awkwardly as they waited.

"I think you were a bit strong with him," Abigail's father said.

"Rubbish," she snapped back. "Every now and then you have to stand up to people."

"But you don't have to be rude," he said. "Sometimes I

wonder if those bankers you work with are having a bad influence on you. I don't have a good impression of them."

"They're perfectly okay, Dad."

Five minutes later Dmitri returned. "Madam, I have good news. One of our parties had booked three tables, but we have persuaded them to squeeze onto two instead."

"Good," Abigail said, raising an eyebrow at her father.

"The table will take a few moments to prepare. Could I recommend you have a drink first?"

Dmitri led the two of them into a room with a wooden bar at one end, an open fire at the other, and in between them an array of armchairs and sofas with guests talking in low voices. The walls were lined with books and in the corners of the room, marble busts sat on tall stone columns.

"I will serve you personally this evening," Dmitri said as he gestured for Abigail and her father to sit. He offered them drinks menus and Abigail ordered a glass of champagne for herself and a gin and tonic for her father. With their drinks served, Dmitri handed them food and wine menus. "Let me know if you would like to order before you move into the dining room," he said.

Abigail's father reached for his drink and caught sight of his watch as it emerged from under his cuff. He stopped and undid the strap so that he could look at it more closely.

"Do you like it?" his daughter asked.

"It's beautiful. Do you know how old it is?"

"The jewellers said it was from the 1940s. Maybe seventy years old?"

"They don't build things like this anymore do they? Seventy years old and still going strong."

"Like you then Dad," Abigail winked at him.

The watch had come into her possession two weeks earlier in a bar in Notting Hill, and her first instinct had been to sell it. A jewellers near her office had told her a little about the Breitling, and said it was worth four thousand pounds. In the end, she had decided not to sell it. Instead, she had given it to her father as a gift earlier that evening.

"It's truly lovely," he said as he strapped it back on. "An antique like this always makes me wonder who's owned it in the past. You know, all the hands it's passed through."

"I knew you'd like it. Personally, I find it too old-fashioned. I can appreciate the craftsmanship, but it was made for a different generation."

"You always were a modern girl," her father nodded.

"I just find antiques depressing. There's something lonely about them, as if they've lost touch with the world around them."

"You can't hide from the past."

"That's not what I'm saying Dad."

"I think you do hide sometimes, I think you try to blot out your roots."

"No I don't," Abigail shook her head.

"It's okay. I can understand that. You want to move up in the world. But everything's built on the past."

"So said the history teacher…"

"Time's precious dear, you only get so much of it. And I want you to be happy. If you don't accept where you've come from, you don't have the foundation to build a future."

"Yes, Dad," Abigail sighed and picked up the menu. "Speaking of the future, shall I order for us? I hope you're feeling hungry, because I'm going to order a lot."

"Don't make it too rich, Abi."

"Come on, Dad. You don't do this very often. I'm going to order lots of courses, but just small portions of each, like a tasting menu." When Dmitri returned, Abigail had made her choices. She chose six courses, and three bottles of wine to accompany them.

"We won't drink three bottles will we?" her father asked.

"We won't finish them, but that doesn't matter."

"It seems a bit wasteful."

"Don't worry Dad, it's on Philip and Avalon Capital, remember? Anyway, you can't have the same bottle of wine with each course. They have to match the food."

The dining room was long and surprisingly grand after the

cosiness of the bar. The floor was an expanse of black and white marble tiles while the ceiling was ornate and arched and looked like the inside of a ribbed white barrel. Renaissance-style frescos decorated the walls, but the tables and chairs were simple, as if from a Parisian bistro.

Dmitri led them through the diners and helped them into their seats. He brought the first bottle of wine, a 1996 Bollinger R.D. extra brut champagne, and then served them Oscietra caviar. The champagne was crisp and dry, full of citrus and nuts that went perfectly with the smooth butteriness of the caviar.

The second course was a plate of poached oysters served in their shells and drizzled with a champagne sabayon sauce. The rich reduction of wine, butter, shallots, egg yolks and oyster juice was exquisite, and as Abigail savoured it, she felt her tension from earlier in the evening evaporate as easily as the food dissolved on her tongue.

Next came a bottle of 2000 Château Figeac, a rich St. Emilion Grand Cru Bordeaux, full of plum and chocolate and cherries and pleasurable warmth. With it, they were served a dish of sliced roast pigeon breast on a bed of chanterelles and mashed potato in a red wine reduction. After that came a course of duck ravioli with a wild mushroom sauce.

"Is everything to your satisfaction?" Dmitri asked as he cleared away their plates.

"It's lovely," Abigail's father replied. Dmitri smiled approvingly as he recognised a glow of contentment creeping over the two of them.

The final bottle was a 2001 Château d'Yquem dessert wine, and at £850 the most expensive of the three. As Abigail held up her glass, the colour of the wine alone, a rich golden honey, caused her to beam with pleasure. Then there were the aromas, of caramelised sugar and lemon and melon and apple, and finally the sweet, sweet taste. It was the crowning glory of the meal. She and her father ate mille-feuille with pears and caramel sauce and pistachios, and tucked into soft French cheeses, but such dishes were just background scenery, mere context for the greatness of the wine.

By the end of the meal, Abigail and her father sat slumped in their seats, their eyes glassy and their movements slow. It was nearly midnight and the dining room had emptied noticeably, save for three or four tables. Dmitri came over and asked if they wanted anything else.

"No, thank you," Abigail said, rousing herself, "I think we should go."

"Was everything to your satisfaction?"

"Very much so," Abigail nodded. "I shan't want to eat anything for a week."

"Yes," her father grunted, "the best meal I think I've ever had."

"Good, then I will fetch the bill," Dmitri said, waving his hand to another waiter across the room.

"Do we need to sign it?" Abigail asked.

"Madam?"

"I suppose we need to sign it so you can charge it to Avalon's account?"

"I don't understand?" Dmitri said.

Abigail picked up her bag and pulled out the letter that she had shown Dmitri earlier that evening. "Here," she said, opening it and handing it to Dmitri. "I expect you need to hold onto that. Do we need to sign the bill so that you can get paid?"

"Madam," Dmitri said, "this letter is no good here."

"What do you mean, no good? I showed it to you before we ate."

"You did, madam, that is correct."

"You said it was current?"

"That is also correct."

"I don't understand?"

"Madam, this letter entitles you to a free meal at L'Oeuf."

"Exactly…"

"But this restaurant is not L'Oeuf. This restaurant is L'Oeuvre."

"L'Oeuvre?"

"Yes, madam, it means 'masterpiece' or 'work of art' in French."

"It can't be…"

"L'Oeuf is close by, but it's on the other side of the street."

"You mean we're in the wrong restaurant?"

A waiter arrived at the table and handed a leather wallet to Dmitri, who then placed it in front of Abigail. She opened the wallet and stared at the bill in front of her.

"This is for £2,914?"

"Yes, madam," Dmitri nodded. "Service is not included."

"But I can't pay this?"

"Surely madam has a credit card?"

"Not with any room on it."

"Perhaps sir could pay?"

"He's a retired school teacher," Abigail exclaimed, "on a paltry state pension."

"I don't suppose we could do the washing up?" Her father suggested.

"That would take many days of work to cover this bill, sir."

"I'm not doing the bloody washing up," Abigail said, staring at her father.

"Then…" her father looked at his daughter, before unbuckling his watch. "What about if I give you this?" He offered the Breitling to Dmitri. "Would that cover the bill?"

"Dad, you can't. It was a present."

"I know dear, but we don't have any other way to pay."

"Let me see," Dmitri said, holding the watch up to the light and examining it. "Gold is it? It's a bit irregular, but I suppose it will do." He turned and smiled at Abigail. "It seems the Greeks aren't the only ones living beyond their means."

3

MARCH: MOMENT OF TRUTH

Richard Day stood in a glass-fronted box up in the stands at Cheltenham racetrack and looked out at the view before him. Immediately in front were throngs of race-goers, a chaotic, swirling sea of tweed suits and hats and binoculars and women wrapped in coats, with fascinators in their hair. Beyond them lay the track itself, a river of green between banks of white rails. And in the distance rose the mass of Cleeve Hill that looked down on the racetrack and gave Cheltenham racecourse its famous amphitheatre feel.

The noise and conviviality of the crowd outside were clearly audible inside the box and added to Richard's sense of wellbeing. It was Gold Cup Day, the final day of the Cheltenham Festival, and he and thirty guests had been treated to a lunch of roast ham and apple crumble and rich Somerset cheese. The third race of the afternoon had finished a few minutes earlier and Richard and his fellow guests had watched from the box drinking red wine and Guinness as the horses flashed past in a streak of pounding muscle and luminous silk.

Many of the guests had returned to the bar or their tables, and some of them had gone to collect winnings from the betting booth outside, but Richard stood watching the empty track. He hadn't bet on the race. He was saving himself for the main event, the Cheltenham Gold Cup itself. A pit of excitement gnawed at his stomach. He couldn't help but feel confident that he was going to win. The past eight days had been some of the luckiest he could remember. He just needed his run of good fortune to hold for one more afternoon.

Richard traced the curve of the track outside, mentally leaping the fences of tightly bound birch sticks that lay across its path like giant shoe brushes. He was sure his horse would come in. How could it not after the week he'd had? He thought back over recent events. It had all started on the Wednesday of the previous week.

Richard lived in Gloucester, six miles up the road. He was thirty-eight years old and worked as the news editor of *The Gloucestershire Chronicle*. He wrote about the minutiae of his county, from road accidents and crime to local politics and business to summer fetes and beauty pageants. Richard saw great value in his role and was proud of his work. He felt passionately about the importance of the press. Information and news were the lifeblood of any community, they glued it together. At the same time, they kept society open, transparent and honest. The press ensured that sunlight shone into even the shadiest corners to root out corruption.

It wasn't always glamorous, but Richard had notched up some notable triumphs over the years. Among his proudest moments were a set of stories exposing a local character called Graham Grubb. For as long as Richard could remember he'd disliked him.

Grubb was a former hero of Gloucester Rugby Club where he'd played for many seasons as a flanker. To his fans, he was remembered as a man of passion and strength, a hard-drinking champion who never hesitated to put his body on the line in the name of his club. To others, he was considered a bully and a cheat, happy to throw punches in the ruck and stamp on opponents on the floor.

He'd played his last game for Gloucester in 1999, and in

the years since had built up a collection of businesses, including a plant hire firm leasing diggers and trucks, and a chain of four garages—Grubb's Garages. He ran a construction company, had a share in a local golf course, and provided various services to the local council. Most famously, he was the co-owner of Shakers, a seamy nightclub known for its fights and the stench of vomit and urine that cloaked the road outside on Sunday mornings.

Grubb, now in his late-forties, was a flamboyant character who had used his local fame and connections to good effect. He lived in a showy manor on the outskirts of Gloucester, drove a Porsche 911 and smoked Cohiba cigars. He ran the London Marathon every year, always ensuring that everyone knew how much money he had raised for charity. His firm organised and sponsored an annual golf competition, and he was still heavily involved with his old rugby club.

The first few times that Richard had met Grubb, he had been struck by the man's aloof arrogance. Grubb had a habit of looking through people as if they didn't count, and dismissing their opinions as worthless. Grubb would give the impression of listening to someone, but then leave mid-way through their anecdote, or else make a comment of his own that was unconnected to the conversation. Richard regarded him as coarse and uncultured, with little interest in anything other than rugby, drinking and lewd humour. Grubb liked to be the centre of attention, he liked an entourage, and Richard always felt uneasy whenever he was around.

Over the years, Richard had taken pleasure in using his newspaper to bring the man down to earth. In one series of stories, Richard had written about an ongoing investigation into Grubb's business for tax evasion. In another run of headlines, the buyers of one of his housing developments had complained of windows falling out of their frames and of blocked drains that leaked sewage. His plant hire business had recorded a string of accidents, including one instance where an employee—who the police discovered was drunk—had driven a flat-bed trailer with a digger on the back into a low bridge.

Some years ago, one of Grubb's ventures, a snooker hall, had burned to the ground, causing suspicion among the loss adjusters sent to evaluate his insurance claim.

Richard had covered these and many other developments in *The Gloucestershire Chronicle*. To him, they pointed to the true character of Grubb, a disreputable man who cut corners and cheated his way through life, intimidating the weak, conning the gullible and trading on his sporting past. But none of *The Chronicle's* stories about Grubb compared to the one that Richard had printed the previous week.

It had been late in the evening, with Richard out walking his dog, when a call came through on his mobile phone. It was from Jim, a photographer who had worked with Richard on *The Chronicle* for several years before moving to London. These days he worked for a paparazzi agency, door-stepping celebrities and hanging around law courts, nightclubs and airports.

Jim had been working that Wednesday night and was camped outside a bar in Mayfair, his teeth chattering with the cold as he spoke to Richard. He was on the trail of a footballer but had seen Grubb arrive at the same bar. Peering through the bar's windows Jim could see Grubb sitting at a table with a young blonde woman who wasn't his wife. They were drinking and talking and "canoodling" as Jim described it. He had called to see if Richard wanted any pictures of Grubb and his "mystery woman".

Richard had been unsure at first. He wasn't in the habit of running such salacious news in the paper. But it didn't take much for Jim to persuade him. Grubb was a figure in the public eye, who used his name and reputation as a local hero to win business and gain influence. Those who dealt with him had a right to know what type of person he was.

Richard had negotiated a fee with Jim and the following morning an email was waiting for him with the pictures attached. They were everything that Jim had said they would be. The first ones were taken through the window of the bar, but later on Jim had snapped Grubb and his woman out on the street, kissing under a street lamp, holding hands, and entering a nearby hotel. The pictures were crisp and clear, and left little doubt that Grubb was having an affair.

The story wrote itself, and Richard loaded the piece with all his best tabloid jargon, of a "secret tryst", a "mystery mistress", a "local rugby star playing away from home", and "the anguish it was sure to cause his wife and family". The only hard part was calling Grubb himself to hear his side of the story.

At first Grubb had been furious, threatening all kinds of retribution, including burning *The Gloucestershire Chronicle* to the ground. Richard had enjoyed that part of the call. But as the conversation progressed, Grubb had softened and pleaded with Richard not to publish, for the sake of his family. He had shown real contrition that caused Richard to waver. It was the first time Richard had felt anything other than dislike for the man, the first time he had seen a human side. But it wasn't enough, not when measured against the years of arrogance and greed and self-promotion, not when set against the history of trampling on the weak and sneering at the rules of fair play and decency.

The story had come out on Friday morning and caused quite a stir. Hard copies of the paper had sold out across Gloucester, and visits to *The Chronicle's* website had soared. Many people congratulated Richard on the story and shared their satisfaction that someone had shown Grubb for the person he really was.

"Did you have anything on that race?" a portly woman in her fifties, dressed in a drab trouser suit, joined Richard at the window. He had met her over lunch at his table. Her name was Chloe Green. She worked in the IT industry, and had grown noticeably voluble the more wine she had drunk.

"No, I'm saving myself for the big one," Richard said.

"The Gold Cup? Which horse?"

"Synchronised. I'm told he's a sure thing."

"What are the odds?"

"About nine to one…"

"Doesn't sound like a sure thing."

"He's not the favourite, but my sports editor gave me the tip. He's obsessed with racing."

"I hope he's right."

"Me too," Richard said, "but I'm feeling good about it. I'm on a bit of a lucky streak at the moment."

"Ah, I see," Chloe said, feigning a frown, "now, I'm worried for you."

"It's true. Sometimes you hit a run of luck and you just have to go with the flow."

Getting a lucky break with the Grubb story had been just the start of Richard's good fortune. On Monday he had played squash after work as he always did, and on leaving the sports centre he had found a gold Breitling watch lying on the pavement. It was clearly an antique and looked expensive. He'd taken it home and showed it to his wife, Mary.

Richard had been taken by the inscription on the back, "May your brief candle shine brightly". With the publication of his recent story about Grubb's affair, Richard felt his own candle was shining more brightly than ever, and deep in his sub-conscious where superstitions lay, he registered the finding of the watch as an omen. He had wanted to keep it. Mary, however, had said it didn't suit him and that he should find out what it was worth.

The following day, Richard had taken it to a jewellers and traded it for two thousand pounds. He'd given half to Mary, and the other half was tucked into his jacket pocket. He was planning to put a large part of it on Synchronised in the Gold Cup.

"It's funny how the world is obsessed with speed isn't it?" Chloe said as Richard patted his jacket pocket to make sure his money was still where he'd put it.

"What do you mean?"

"Like these races," she gestured out towards the track, causing her wine to slosh over the side of her glass. "Everything's about who can do things in the shortest amount of time."

"That's the point of a race isn't it?"

"But everything in life is becoming a race. Who's got the quickest horse, who's got the fastest car, which company can get its products to market first, which bank can execute its trades the fastest."

"I suppose you're right…" Richard nodded

"Your industry's the same. The media's all about who can break a story first and fastest. My industry too."

"Computers?"

"Sure," she nodded. "It never ends. Who can build the fastest processors. Who can handle the most operations per second. The speeds go up year after year, month after month."

"Life's a competition…" Richard shrugged.

"True," Chloe said, "and time is how we measure the winners."

"You sound depressed by it all."

"No," Chloe shook her head, "but I do envy the people who don't compete on speed, the gymnasts, the musicians, the novelists. The rest of us are on a treadmill, and it's speeding up. The world keeps getting quicker and quicker. People don't walk through life anymore, they sprint, and if you can't keep up, you're out of the race."

"The rat race…"

"Exactly."

"I blame your industry," Richard smiled. "Computers are the reason why everything is speeding up. How do newspapers keep up with the internet and Twitter and all the other technologies out there?"

"Touché," she smiled, and looked at her watch. "Have you placed your bet yet?"

"No, I should get going."

"Here," Chloe said, handing Richard a twenty pound note. "Put that on Synchronised for me would you?"

"Sure," he nodded, and headed out to the betting ring where most of the bookmakers were offering odds of eight to one. It was a little less generous than he had hoped, but nonetheless acceptable. He wasn't sure how much money to put down. He'd contemplated putting his full thousand on the race, with the prospect of winning eight times that amount. In the end, though, he felt too anxious. Despite his confidence, he decided on five hundred pounds. If he won, the payout would be exciting, but if he lost he still had half his money left.

Back in the box, Richard gave Chloe her betting slip and paced about with nervous excitement. Several other members of the party had joined the two of them at the window and were surveying the scene through binoculars. Richard had left his own pair at home and cursed his forgetfulness.

Those binoculars had been the third piece of good luck to strike him, after the Grubb story and the gold watch. A parcel had arrived in the office for Richard on Tuesday afternoon, a cardboard box with an envelope glued to the top. The envelope contained an invitation to lunch and an afternoon of races at the Cheltenham Gold Cup. The organiser of the lunch was a chain of fitness centres called Trim, Toned & Terrific that was planning to open branches across the county. Richard wasn't interested in their plans, but he was happy to help them celebrate.

Inside the cardboard box that had come with the invitation, Richard had found a rucksack emblazoned with the gym's logo, and inside the rucksack a pair of Nikon binoculars, a bottle of Jameson 18-year-old Master Selection whiskey, and a rich woollen scarf—everything a race-goer needed. Richard often received invitations to launches and events and ceremonies from organisations looking to create publicity. But he had never seen one as lavish as this.

"I see you brought your binoculars with you," Richard said to Chloe, "did they come with your invitation?"

"Yes," she nodded, looking through them across the track. "Generous of them wasn't it?"

"You'll have to tell me what you see. I left my pair at home."

"They're getting ready to start. What does our horse look like?"

"He's number ten, look on the saddle."

"I can't see. There's too many of them."

"Look for a jockey wearing green and gold hoops on his jersey. Those are the colours of JP McManus."

"He's the jockey is he?" Chloe asked.

"No, the owner. The jockey is Tony McCoy. Jockeys always wear the owner's colours."

A minute later, the race commentator announced that they were off. Richard could see the pack of horses picking up speed. Ahead of them lay a course that covered three miles and two-and-a-half furlongs, and included twenty-two fences. It would take around seven minutes to complete. Seven minutes of nerves and anxiety. Richard felt his heart pounding in his chest as he listened to the commentary. The early leaders were Midnight Chase, Kauto Star, Time for Rupert and Knockara Beau.

"They're at the second fence now, oh and there's a faller," the commentator gasped. "What A Friend is down. What A Friend is a faller at fence two."

"Did any other horses get caught up?" Richard asked, straining his eyes to see.

"No," Chloe said as she watched through her binoculars. "Only one horse down, but I still can't see Synchronised. He's not one of the front-runners."

"Don't worry, the pack's the best place to be. He's just keeping pace at this stage, it's a long race."

By now, the horses were riding the "long, lingering run down the hill" as the commentator described it, before turning into the home stretch with its up-hill incline where the horses streamed past Richard's box. This was just the first lap of the race. There was another to go, and as they flashed by, Richard caught sight of Synchronised, perhaps in ninth or tenth place at the back of the pack.

"We're pretty much last," Chloe said, looking up from her binoculars.

"It's okay, there's still more than half the race to go," Richard replied, more for his own benefit than for Chloe's.

The horses thundered on, looping away from the

grandstand, and Richard followed Synchronised, unable to look away, but consumed with a growing fear that his horse was failing him. Fence after fence, Synchronised barely improved his position.

"As they turn back towards home now, Time for Rupert is still out in front, from The Giant Bolster in second," the commentator sang out. "Long Run is just holding in third. Burton Port is on the outside, trying to improve. Synchronised once again is just found wanting for pace."

"Come on Synchronised," Chloe yelled, her binoculars glued to her face. "He could still do it."

"Two fences from home, The Giant Bolster moves to the lead in the Cheltenham Gold Cup from Time for Rupert, and Long Run. Burton Port made a challenge but can't go on. Synchronised with the white face for Tony McCoy is coming home strongly." Richard closed his eyes, and listened to the commentator. He couldn't bear to watch it himself.

"Over the last and Synchronised has fought his way to the front," the commentator's voice had grown loud and breathless. "Long Run is battling on the far side. The Giant Bolster is in there too. But it's Synchronised who has come right from the back of the field. Tony McCoy has timed his finish perfectly, and it's Synchronised who crosses first to win a dramatic Gold Cup victory."

Richard opened his eyes. The crowd out in front of his box had erupted into frantic cheering and urging. Richard's heart was pounding so heavily his ribs felt like they might crack under the pressure. Chloe threw down her binoculars, punched the air, and hugged Richard with delight.

"I told you I'm on a lucky streak," Richard shouted with excitement. "What a race, eh?"

"Brilliant," Chloe nodded, "although hardly a sure thing."

"It was a bit close wasn't it!" Richard exhaled, and checked his betting slip to confirm his win. "I'm not sure my heart can take much more of that."

Richard went outside to collect his winnings—four thousand pounds, on top of his original stake. For a journalist, it was a small fortune. Had he ever had a better week, he wondered? The exposé of Grubb on Friday, the discovery of the gold watch on Monday, the lavish gifts and invitation from Trim, Toned & Terrific on Tuesday, and now a jackpot on the horses at the Gold Cup. And that wasn't even considering his trip to London on Wednesday.

As he queued to collect his winnings, Richard thought back to the night he'd spent in the capital. He'd caught the train there early that morning to take part in a conference in Earls Court. The Third Annual European Media Forum was a two-day gathering of people from the continent's media industries, from television and radio to newspapers and magazines. Richard had been invited to speak as part of a panel debating the future of local newspapers. Amid falling circulation and the rise of digital technology, how could local newspapers survive?

The session was lively and well attended and afterwards Richard had joined his fellow panellists in a bar in the conference centre. The place was full of journalists and publishers and TV producers and it was there that he had met Adalia, a Spanish woman who ran a news website in Seville. Adalia had said how much she enjoyed Richard's comments in the debate and wanted to hear more.

She was exactly how Richard would have imagined such a woman, with dark Andalucian features, a slender figure and a cascade of black curls. Her dress was professional—a black skirt and jacket over a crimson red shirt—and her manner earnest. She listened with intensity, her face full of concentration. Occasionally she laughed, but mostly she was focused and serious, plying Richard with questions in her Spanish accent, and never revealing much of herself. She was a little younger than Richard, perhaps in her early thirties, but she projected a sophistication that he found intoxicating.

At 9.00pm, Richard announced that he was leaving to catch his train home, but Adalia pleaded with him to stay instead and carry on talking. She had a room in the Rembrandt Hotel in Knightsbridge, they could go there and open some wine. There was so much more that she wanted to know. Richard protested that he had to get back to Gloucester, but inside his head he knew he would stay. He called Mary and explained that the conference had run late, he was spending the night in London and would catch the first train back in the morning.

The two of them had taken a taxi to the Rembrandt where Adalia ordered hummus and babaganoush and feta cheese salad from room service and a bottle of Rioja. They ate and drank and talked, and as the night wore on, they had ended up in bed together.

The next day, as Richard made his way home, he had reflected on his encounter with Adalia. It was the first time he had been with another woman since marrying Mary three years earlier, and he was surprised at how little guilt he felt. Perhaps it was because the betrayal was purely physical. Emotionally he had stayed true to Mary. Adalia was returning home to Seville and he to Gloucester. They would never see each other again.

Or perhaps his lack of guilt confirmed one of Richard's deeper suspicions, that society had somehow organised itself at odds with human nature. Even a casual glance through any tabloid newspaper would show how humans struggled to stay faithful to just one partner. Maybe society had set itself an impossible set of rules that needed re-writing to reflect the true mating habits of the human species.

Richard reached the front of the queue to the betting booth, and as he counted his winnings, he felt overcome with euphoria. A week this good needed celebrating. He felt the need to share his elation with others. Several of Richard's friends were also at the Festival, in a different part of the ground, and Richard decided to call them when he returned to the box. His newspaper had two journalists on duty at the race track, and Richard would call them too. Tonight had to be a party, a celebration of his good fortune.

Back in the box, Richard found it fuller than when he left. The tables were full of the same people who had eaten lunch, but now others were standing around them too. Richard found his seat and asked Chloe what was happening.

"There's a speech or something about to happen," she explained. "The owner of Trim, Toned & Terrific."

"Who is the owner?" Richard asked. But before Chloe could reply, he saw for himself.

Grubb strode in through the door in an open-neck shirt and jacket, waving to people in the room that he knew, his face set with its usual half-smile. Several people in the audience whooped and clapped and Grubb stood for a moment, absorbing his reception before quieting the room down.

"I hope my team have been treating you well," he began. "I hope the horses have been treating you well."

"Did you know that Grubb was the owner?" Richard whispered to Chloe. He pulled the invitation card from his jacket pocket and checked it—there was no mention of Grubb on it.

"Of course," she nodded. "He got the franchise for the gym from some American company."

Richard was confused. Why had Grubb invited him? Could it have been an error by his PR team? Richard doubted it. Was it an olive branch? Was his invitation a gesture of peace with *The Chronicle* after all the years of negative reporting?

Grubb continued with his speech, and had clearly seen Richard sitting at one of the tables. But his face gave nothing away. A wink or a smile might have suggested reconciliation. A frown might have suggested that a mistake had been made. But instead, Richard felt nothing from him.

When the speech was over, and Grubb had told everyone about his plans for Trim, Toned & Terrific, the crowd stood and clapped him and raised toasts in his honour. Richard's sense of elation had long since given way to one of concern. The whole room seemed to be Grubb supporters and Richard felt isolated in their company. At the first opportunity, he grabbed his coat and made for the door.

"Hey there, reporter," Richard felt a hand on his shoulder. He turned and found Grubb just inches from his face. "Before you run off, could I have a word with you?"

"About what?"

"I've got something I want to show you, it'll only take a minute."

"What is it?"

"Let's walk outside and get away from these people. Maybe the Parade Ring." They walked in silence, Grubb just a step behind Richard. The crowds by the Parade Ring were still thick and loud, but Grubb found a quiet spot away from the bustle.

"What is it? What did you want to show me?" Richard asked.

"You think you're quite righteous, don't you?" Grubb said.

"I don't…"

"All of you at *The Chronicle*," Grubb continued, "you think you're some kind of police force… You're all about trying to keep society in line, that's how you see yourselves, isn't it?"

"We provide a public service, if that's what you mean." Richard felt vulnerable. It occurred to him that Grubb might try to hit him.

"My problem is, who polices the police? You set yourselves up as self-appointed guardians of public morals, but who polices the media?"

"There are organisations… the Press Complaints Commission for one."

"Obviously they do a lousy bloody job."

"If you have a complaint about our reporting, then you're welcome to submit it…"

"No, I have a complaint about you," Grubb reached into his pocket and pulled out a piece of paper that he unfolded and smoothed out on his jacket. "You sit behind your journalistic principles, all high and mighty, washing everyone else's dirty laundry in public. But what about you?"

"What about me?"

"What about your own dirty laundry? Whose job is it to wash your laundry in public?"

"I don't understand."

"Read this," Grubb said, handing over the piece of paper. "I thought I'd have a go at being a news publisher myself. That there is my first edition. Probably my only edition, but who knows. I've called it *Retribution*."

Richard took the paper. His stomach weakened and he felt the urge to vomit. The A3 page had been designed like a newspaper, with the masthead, *Retribution*, printed across the top next to a stylised logo. A colour picture took up half of the page—it was a photograph of Richard and Adalia in flagrante in her hotel room. Her eyes had been blacked out, but Richard's face was clearly visible as they lay together naked on the bed. The story next to the picture began: "Married Gloucester journalist Richard Day was caught romping with a mystery woman in a London hotel room on Wednesday."

"When you ran that story about me last week, I wished dearly that I could go back and undo what I'd done," Grubb said. "I felt so guilty. But that's the thing about time isn't it? It only moves in one direction. So as I was wallowing in my guilt, I began to think about the role of the press. I thought, if the press is the guardian of public morals, then who keeps a check on the morals of our media? So I set you three tests. To be honest, I didn't expect you to fail quite so easily."

"What tests?"

"I've had you followed all week. On Monday, after your squash game, my guy left a gold watch on the pavement. He was waiting for you outside and placed it just before you came out of the squash courts. You know, an honest person would have handed it in to the sports centre, or the police. But what did you do? You sold it and pocketed the cash."

"I'll get it back for you…"

"There's no need."

"Really, I can buy it back from the shop…"

"Don't worry, it didn't mean anything to me. I'm part-owner of a restaurant in London and a customer used it to pay for their dinner," Grubb shrugged. "The point, though, is that you did the dishonourable thing. You'll find that story on page two if you open it up. So that was the first test. The second one came on Tuesday. Your newspaper has a policy on accepting gifts doesn't it? What is it? Anything with a value of more than twenty pounds has to be returned to the giver?"

"Yes," Richard nodded.

"All in the name of protecting editorial integrity and independence—and quite right too. We can't have our journalists accepting anything that might be considered a bribe. But you ignored that rule didn't you? The rucksack from my gym and all the stuff inside was worth at least four hundred pounds. That's a decent bottle of whisky, and those binoculars are expensive too. We've covered that story on page three."

Richard opened the paper—it was just four pages, the outside covers and an inside spread. Page two carried the headline, "*Chronicle* news editor makes off with valuable watch", and beneath it was the story and a photograph of the Breitling. On page three were pictures of the invitation to the Gold Cup, the bottle of whisky and the binoculars, and of Richard walking home with the rucksack slung over his shoulder.

"The third test… well, you saw that on the cover," Grubb continued. "My people found out about your conference in London. We arranged for an escort to pick you up. You remember Adalia? Lovely girl I'm told. She certainly looks it in the pictures."

"You set me up?"

"Three times, and you failed on each occasion. So there we have it: theft, greed and dishonesty, and sexual deviancy—an insight into the moral fibre of our noble press corps. The back page is an editorial. You should read it when you get a chance. It's all about hypocrisy and privacy and the role of the press."

"What are you going to do with this?"

"It's already done. I've printed 15,000 copies. There should be a few thousand floating around the bars here at the racetrack later on. I've got a team distributing them down on the High Street in Cheltenham, and back home in Gloucester too. Of course, I made sure one was sent to Mary, so that might take a bit of explaining later on. I was going to give you a right to reply in my paper, but it's probably best if you explain yourself directly to Mary."

Grubb looked up at the blanket of low cloud that hung heavily in the sky. A squall of wind gusted through the Parade Ring and caught the paper in Richard's hands, sending it cartwheeling into the crowd.

"Not the best of weather is it?" Grubb said, turning up the collar on his jacket. "Still, I feel in a surprisingly good mood. Enjoy the rest of the races." And with that he strode away.

4

APRIL: TIME IS MONEY

Norman Greenwich sat down at the kitchen table where his wife Catherine was eating toast and listening to the news on the radio. The night had bruised into the purples of dawn and the day was gathering light and life.

"Where's Susan?" Norman asked, as he poured himself tea and reached for the toast rack.

"She's getting ready," Catherine said.

"As long as she isn't late."

"School doesn't start for another hour and a half."

"Punctuality is a habit, and habits are best formed young." Norman buttered his toast, spreading the butter evenly to all four edges and all four corners. The marmalade was harder to apply with the same evenness, given the chunks of rind that refused any kind of smooth distribution, but as long as the depth of the spread was as uniform as possible then Norman was content.

"You know today's one of my Gloucester days," he said, "so I won't be home until 8.30 this evening."

"What about Susan's new shoes?"

"What about them?"

"We discussed it yesterday. You know she needs them. I thought I'd take her today and get some."

"How much?"

"About forty pounds."

"Forty pounds on shoes for a nine-year-old?" Norman pulled out his wallet. "Here's thirty. And remember to keep the receipt."

After breakfast, Norman left his house at exactly 7.00am and caught the bus to Bristol Temple Meads train station. At 7.22am he was standing on the platform, and at 7.30am his train was pulling out of the station on its way to Gloucester. Norman smiled inwardly. He had plenty to be happy about.

The prompt running of a train always put him in a good mood. Seeing a complex system like a railway operating to plan filled him with a profound satisfaction. He imagined armies of planners and workers who shared his passion for order and timeliness. He pictured people of principle, who took pride in their work, and who stood against the creeping wave of laziness, lateness and slapdashness that was embracing society.

Then there was the spring morning. As the train gathered speed through the suburbs and raced out into the countryside, the views were a riot of budding green leaves. Norman looked out and saw horse chestnut and hazel, and hornbeam and beech. Scruffy hedgerows were full of ash and may trees, while out in the fields stood stout oaks, perhaps as old as the railway itself. As Norman took it in, he found himself reciting Robert Browning: "O to be in England, now that April's there…" Nature had its own timetable too.

Such pleasures never failed to lift Norman's spirits. But today, there was another reason for feeling giddy. Today he planned to do something that was most out of character. He felt a little guilty at the prospect, but his excitement was far greater.

Norman worked as an accountant at Bristol & Gloucester Insurance. He was based in the company's main office in Bristol, but every fortnight he made the hour-long train journey to Gloucester to spend the day running through the accounts of the office there.

It was a fifteen-minute walk from Gloucester train station to the office, which meant that Norman was usually at his desk with a mug of tea and ready to begin his day by 8.50am. For the past two visits, however, Norman hadn't started until 9.00am. Along his route was a small jewellers called Moon & Sons. Norman always smiled when he saw the shop's nameplate, and occasionally he would stop to look at the antique watches in their windows, just for a minute or so.

But two fortnights earlier, one watch in particular had caught his attention and caused him to linger a little longer than usual. The watch was a Breitling Chronomat from 1946, made from rose-coloured gold. Norman had seen a similar watch once before. Back in 1998, the chairman of Bristol & Gloucester Insurance had left after forty years of service, and the firm had given him an identical watch for his retirement. Norman had been entrusted to keep it in the company's petty cash safe in the days before it was presented to the chairman, and during those days he had taken a strong fancy to the timepiece.

The face itself showed the time in hours, minutes and seconds, and two smaller dials showed minutes and seconds for the stopwatch. But what had really intrigued Norman were the slide-rule functions. Around the edge of the watch face ran a logarithmic scale, and around this, inscribed on the rotating bezel, ran a second scale. In an age before computers, mathematicians could use it to compute complex calculations by twisting the bezel and matching different points on the two concentric scales. It was, in effect, a sophisticated analogue computer, capable of determining speeds, distances, interest rates, percentages and much else besides.

To Norman, the watch stood for old-fashioned values, of reliability, quality and precision. It was stylish, yet highly functional too. It represented an age of thoroughness and elegance, when people understood how to solve a maths problem from first principles rather than by using a digital calculator.

Norman had envied the chairman for his retirement gift at the time, but had forgotten about it in the years since—until four weeks earlier. Seeing the exact same watch for sale in the window of Moon & Sons had re-stoked his dormant desires. On his two previous trips to Gloucester, Norman had visited the shop during his lunch break to look at the watch more closely. He had held it and felt its solid, well-crafted weight. He had tested the stop/start buttons of the stopwatch and watched the hands respond with their one fifth of a second accuracy. But most of all, he had tested the rotating slide rule, calculating exchange rates and productivity equations, and doing difficult divisions.

Every day for the past four weeks, the watch had played on Norman's mind. He yearned to have it. But at £3,500, the price was as much as a month's salary. He had a mortgage to service and bills to pay and a wife and daughter to keep in shoes and food. Each year he set himself strict budgets that mapped out his costs for the coming twelve months and allowed him to save a little extra for holidays and for his retirement. There was no way he could afford such an extravagance.

But no matter how much Norman argued with himself and laid out the case for financial prudence, the image of the watch wouldn't leave him. It was like a magnet distorting his thoughts. When he tried to concentrate on his work, his thoughts would drift to the watch. He would imagine wearing it, and how it would feel to be connected to an item of such mathematical and mechanical mastery. And the more that Norman thought about it, the more he believed the watch was somehow an embodiment of all that he himself stood for.

At first Norman had fought all thoughts of acquiring the watch. But slowly, over the previous four weeks, his resolve had lessened and he had begun to calculate ways that he might scrape together the means to buy it. He had a savings account with enough money in it to make the purchase. Catherine would never know because he was the one who managed their financial affairs. If he took out £3,500 for the watch, and then cut back in one or two other areas, he could rebuild his savings and make up for the shortfall.

He could sell his current watch—that would bring in at least a hundred pounds. He had budgeted to buy a new suit in the summer, but could happily buy one the following year instead. He could reduce the budget for their annual holiday in August by a few hundred pounds. The thermostat on the central heating could be adjusted to save on fuel bills. And there was certainly fat that could be trimmed from his regular weekly and monthly expenses.

When he added it all up, Norman was sure that he could repay the money into his savings account within eighteen months. And so he had gradually convinced himself that it was entirely justifiable to buy the watch. He planned to make the purchase today.

As the train pulled into Gloucester station, Norman felt a momentary worry that the watch might have been sold since he was last in town. He rushed out of the station, and only relaxed when he reached Moon & Sons and saw the Breitling in the window just as he had left it a fortnight earlier.

Norman hurried on towards his office, but despite his best efforts to focus on his work, the morning passed frustratingly slowly. By midday, Norman's patience had run out and he left for his lunch break half an hour earlier than usual. He headed straight to Moon & Sons and bought the watch, putting his old watch in his pocket and strapping on the Breitling in its place.

The day had blossomed into radiant warmth and sunshine, and Norman bought a sandwich and sat on a bench beneath a sycamore tree where the spring leaves glowed with youthful verdance. As he ate, he twisted his arm back and forth, admiring the watch as it glinted in the sunlight. Its proportions suited his wrist perfectly, while its understated elegance oozed dignity, and spoke of education and quiet sophistication. Norman felt at ease with the world and deeply happy.

Back at the office, he put the watch into his briefcase for

safe-keeping, and kept it there until he arrived back home. He had thought hard about how to introduce the watch to Catherine. He couldn't admit to his wife that he had bought it. Nor could he admit to finding it on the train—that would require him to hand it over to the lost and found department. Instead, he told Catherine that he had found it in a rubbish bin outside the station.

"In a bin?" she asked when he showed it to her. "What were you doing looking in the bins?"

"I wasn't. I went over to throw away my newspaper and saw something glinting, so I looked closer and there it was."

"What, just sitting on top of the rubbish?"

"Yes, well, it was sitting in one of those polystyrene burger boxes."

"Someone just threw it away?"

"It looked that way."

"But it's gold isn't it?" Catherine held it up to the light. "Why would someone throw it away?"

"Who knows," Norman shrugged. "Maybe there was an argument? Maybe the watch was a gift from a lover, they fell out, and the gift was thrown away."

"How extraordinary. Do you think it's expensive?"

"It could be."

"What will you do with it?"

"I don't know. Maybe I'll wear it."

"It's not as nice as the watch you have now."

"You think?"

"This one looks old... and there's an inscription on the back."

"Yes, I saw that—'May your brief candle shine brightly'."

"It obviously meant something to somebody," Catherine said, turning the watch back over and returning it to her husband. "Do you think you should try to find the person who threw it away?"

"How would I? It's a train station. Thousands of people pass through there everyday."

"You should get it valued."

"Good idea," Norman nodded. "Maybe I'll do it this weekend." He opened his desk drawer and placed the watch carefully inside.

His plan was working well. Catherine believed his story. But he wasn't in the clear just yet. He had to be nonchalant about it for now. He could get the watch valued on the weekend, just to keep up the illusion, and at the same time sell his current watch. It would then be relatively easy to explain that he had lost his old watch and would wear the Breitling as a replacement. Norman closed his desk drawer and reached across for his household accounting ledger.

"Did you get Susan's shoes today?" he asked, opening the book, just as he did every night. Spread across its pages were neat columns of numbers and dates and bank balances itemizing all of the family's expenses.

"We looked, but we couldn't find any for thirty pounds," Catherine said. "The price really is closer to forty pounds."

"Keep looking, and if you absolutely can't find any, then we'll have a re-think."

"I did spend ten of the thirty pounds on petrol, and another five on milk and bread."

"Do you have the receipts?"

"Here," Catherine rummaged through her purse and handed them over.

Norman studied the slips closely, before writing the transactions into his ledger. "It's criminal the price of petrol these days. I just don't believe the government's inflation figures."

"Food prices are just as bad."

"Couldn't you use a cheaper supermarket?"

"Everywhere's expensive these days. You can't get around it."

"You know, I was thinking I might start taking sandwiches to work with me," Norman said. It was a good moment to introduce the idea. Catherine would think it was a response to the rising price of food, but in fact it was part of Norman's plan to reduce his weekly spending in order to pay for the watch. "I've calculated that making sandwiches at home is a good bit cheaper than buying them at work."

"You'll have to give me a bit more money then."

"Of course. But would you mind making sandwiches for me?"

"Not at all," Catherine shrugged.

"Good. Let's start tomorrow."

The following morning, Norman left for work with his sandwiches duly made and neatly stacked in a Tupperware box. He also skipped his usual stop at the newsagent on his street. He could go without his daily paper. Instead, he had decided he would read the copy that was supplied to his office. It wasn't always in the best condition, given that it was shared among the staff, but not buying a paper would save him around two hundred pounds a year.

As Norman boarded his bus without the paper, and with his sandwiches in his briefcase, he felt pleasantly virtuous. He would get his old watch valued during his lunch break, secure a second opinion on the weekend, and then sell it for the highest offer. As soon as that was done, he could wear the Breitling.

Now that he owned the watch, Norman found it much easier to concentrate at work. His thoughts still strayed occasionally to his desk drawer at home and the watch ticking quietly within it. But it wouldn't be long now before it was a permanent feature on his wrist. With that reassuring image, Norman was able to focus wholeheartedly on the accruals and receivables and cash flow projections that made up his daily routine.

At 6.40pm, Norman walked through his front door, just as he did every day. Susan was eating her tea and Catherine was sitting beside her talking about her school play. Norman changed out of his suit and then it was his turn to spend time with his daughter, helping with her homework and coaxing her through the intricacies of long division.

By 8.00pm, Susan was in bed and Catherine was back in the kitchen preparing supper. Norman fetched his ledger from the desk, put it down on the kitchen table, and opened it before him. The page was nearly full and Norman ran his fingers over the neat columns of script. There was something highly satisfying about the feel of a page of hand-written text and numbers. The paper had lost its gloss and smoothness, and instead was rough, crinkled and marked—it had the texture of industry and diligence and conscientiousness.

"Do you have any receipts from today?" Norman asked as he ran his fingers over the pages, stretching them taut.

"I do," Catherine nodded, taking her pan off the stove and wiping her hands on her apron. "Quite an exciting one." She disappeared out of the kitchen and came back a moment later carrying a piece of paper and an envelope.

"What is it?" Norman asked.

"It's a receipt for that watch you found."

"What do you mean a receipt?"

"I was listening to the radio this morning, and they said there was an antiques fair in town. So I took the watch along."

"What for?"

"To get it valued. You'll never believe what they said it was worth," she paused, expecting Norman to show more interest in her endeavours, but he sat completely still, staring at his ledger. "Go on, have a guess," she prompted him, "just take a wild guess."

"Three and a half thousand pounds?" Norman whispered, his stomach tightening. After all, that was the price that he himself had paid for it.

"No, don't be daft," Catherine laughed. "Not that much, but it was a lot. There was a man at the fair from an antiques shop in London. He said it was worth one thousand pounds. Can you believe it? A thousand pounds!"

"You didn't sell it?"

"I did."

Norman closed his eyes and his mind went numb. He wanted to listen to Catherine, he wanted to understand what she had done, but he felt too weak. Instead, his thoughts turned to the previous day when he had sat on the bench under the sycamore tree, eating his sandwich and admiring the glint of the sun on the face of his Breitling.

"Look, here's the receipt," Catherine said, placing it on the table. She opened the envelope and took out a wad of fifty-pound notes. "And here's the money. See? He gave it to me right there and then. Think of what we can do with it. A thousand pounds, and it just fell into our laps out of nowhere."

Norman stared at the money, unable to speak.

"Are you okay dear?" Catherine asked. "You look pale."

"I'm not feeling very well," Norman muttered, pushing back his chair.

"What's wrong? Can I get you something?"

"No, no," Norman struggled to his feet. "I just need to lie down."

"Do you still want dinner?"

"Not tonight, I just need to get to bed."

"Shall I put the money in the desk?"

"Yes," Norman said and staggered out of the kitchen.

Catherine watched him go and felt sad for him. Norman must really be ill, she thought, to show such indifference to their windfall. She tidied up the money and the ledger and put them away in the desk. She looked in on their bedroom and saw Norman standing in front of the sink with his head in his hands.

"Are you sure I can't get you anything," she asked.

"No, nothing."

Catherine closed the bedroom door and returned to the kitchen. She stopped and listened to the sound of the house, and when she was sure that all was quiet, she tugged open the kitchen drawer where she kept clean towels. She slid her fingers underneath them, reached to the back of the drawer and pulled out a second envelope. She opened it and smiled at the second wad of fifty-pound notes inside. She was tempted to pull them out and count them but she thought better of it and tucked the envelope back into its hiding place.

The man at the antiques fair had been kind enough to write a receipt for just half the price that he had paid her for the watch. And so, alongside Norman's one thousand pounds,

Catherine had another thousand to buy shoes for Susan, and perhaps the face cream that Norman always said was too expensive, and possibly one or two other little treats for herself and her daughter. How nice it would be to step out of their financial straitjacket and live a little. Norman would never know. He would be delighted with his own thousand, she was sure of it. He probably just needed a good night's sleep.

5

MAY: TIME FLIES

Gregory Pope closed the door to his office and stared through the glass at the rows of workers sitting at their desks on the other side. They were his team, they reported to him, all sixteen of them, but it didn't feel like that anymore. Over the past few months, Gregory had felt them slipping away from him.

It was his birthday in one day's time, and a year earlier his staff had made a big effort for the occasion. He had overheard their conversations planning which restaurant they should book for a celebratory lunch. He had been proud and satisfied that his staff not only respected him, but that they liked him too and wanted to express their appreciation. The lunch had been a great success. Everyone had drunk too much wine and he had given them all the afternoon off as a gesture of thanks.

This year everything had changed. He sensed no planning at all, not even a glimmer of acknowledgement. He was happy to forget his birthday—fifty-two years was nothing to celebrate. But what bothered him was the strong feeling that he had lost the loyalty of his team, that they had deserted him.

As he watched his staff going about their work, Julian

Cutter walked into the office and Gregory recognised a distinct change in the mood of the team. As Julian made his way through the desks, the workers stopped what they were doing and smiled at him, some of them waved. They all had something to say to him, some small pleasantry or other.

Gregory glanced at his watch. It was 4.00pm—Julian had missed most of the day. He was dressed in unconventional clothes too. It was office policy that everyone must wear a suit, the women too. But Julian was the exception. Today he was wearing a purple silk shirt and tight jeans, with overly pointed shoes on his feet. As he passed Gregory's office, he nodded his head and lifted his briefcase—a garish crocodile skin satchel—as if he were tilting his hat. Gregory forced a smile in return.

Gregory ran a think tank called the Sustainable Planet Foundation. Its purpose was to track the use of natural resources around the world, and to explore how that would shape the future. Global warming and environmental damage were important parts of the research, but so too were questions of how expanding populations and rising economic development could continue in the face of a planet with finite stocks of coal, oil, fish, water and agricultural land. Was humanity doomed to a Malthusian future of famine, plague and war? Or would human inventiveness step in, just as it had on so many occasions throughout history, to save the day?

Gregory felt strongly about the work his team was doing. He was a trained economist and his whole life seemed like preparation for his current role. In his early career, he'd worked in the planning team at Royal Dutch Shell, building long-range scenarios for oil and gas and the issues affecting the industry. Later, he'd joined the Food & Agriculture Organisation of the United Nations, working in their offices in Ghana and Chile, before moving to the head office in Rome. In 2002, he'd joined a boutique bank in London where he worked on investment opportunities in clean energy and environmental protection.

He'd joined the Foundation in 2009 to make a difference. He'd seen the damage that petrochemicals were doing. He'd witnessed the way that agriculture was plundering the earth. Now he wanted to use his experience to put the world onto a more stable footing. He shuddered at how much damage one generation of humanity—a tiny proportion of human history—could inflict. And time was running out.

The think tank was backed by a wealthy Australian called Stanley Steddon. He'd made a fortune in insurance—in the latest "rich list" from Forbes magazine, he was ranked as the 430th wealthiest person in the world, worth US$3 billion. These days he was retired. He lived in Monte Carlo, but had an office in Mayfair in London, just behind Berkeley Square, that managed his financial affairs and housed the Foundation too.

Everything about the man was formal. He insisted that all his staff wore suits. Everyone—even Gregory—addressed him as "Mr Steddon". He demanded a strict "clean desk" policy, with all papers and files tidied away at the end of each day. The office had a fully equipped café, complete with a barista who served tea and coffee in china cups, and wore a white jacket and black trousers that came straight from the British Raj. Anyone eating food at their desk, even a sandwich, had to use a china plate from the kitchen.

Gregory was happy to enforce Mr Steddon's office rules. He felt the formality added focus and gravitas to the think tank and encouraged respect for the work at hand. The staff often joked about the stiffness of their environment, but they were paid well and the work they did was interesting and important.

The one exception to the straight-laced culture was Julian Cutter. He was part of Gregory's team, and yet ignored all the rules. Julian had been hired by Mr Steddon himself seven months earlier. His title was marketing director, and his role was to popularise the work of the Foundation and take it to a wider audience.

"We need the world to know about your research," Mr Steddon had explained to Gregory at the time. "All this analysis is no good if it just sits on a shelf."

Julian had come from a digital marketing agency, and somehow had built a rapport with Mr Steddon that surpassed the trust that Gregory had established. Julian's relationship with Mr Steddon was such that he not only dressed how he liked, and kept his own hours, but he referred to their patron as Stanley, sometimes even as Stan. Nobody else in the team would dare to be so familiar. And yet Mr Steddon seemed to welcome Julian's casual manner, attributing it to the quirkiness of a creative spirit. The rest of the team, though, were academics, scientists, economists and researchers and they had to stick to the rules.

Gregory always made sure that Mr Steddon was updated with their latest research and the reports they wrote. But lately, Gregory sensed that Julian's marketing efforts held greater interest for him. He would ask how many people were visiting their website. What was the strategy for Facebook and Twitter? How was work progressing on a series of short videos aimed at bringing the research to life? When could the Foundation expect to produce a longer film that would rival Al Gore's "An Inconvenient Truth" in its impact?

Gregory recognised the importance of marketing, and agreed that it wasn't enough only to write reports and speak on the conference circuit. Their message needed a bigger stage. But Julian's approach was all wrong. The Foundation's work was complex and detailed, and yet Julian stressed simplicity. In the process, much of the Foundation's research lost its nuance and insight and became bland slogans with little weight for a serious audience.

"People don't read big heavy reports these days," Julian often told Gregory, "you've got to give them the story in pictures."

"If we were selling beer or shampoo then I'd agree with you," Gregory would reply, "but we want to influence governments and investors and companies. We want to influence policymakers. We've got to show more depth."

"Policymakers respond to what the public wants," Julian would argue in return. "You have to influence public opinion first. You have to build from the ground up."

And so their arguments would continue, with Julian

usually finding a supportive ear from Mr Steddon. Julian's most recent idea had been to set up "doomsday clocks" on the internet that counted down to critical points in the future when key resources would be used up if current rates of consumption continued without any change. He'd used work done by Gregory's team to build them, so they were backed by rigorous analysis. But they were also a gross simplification. As Gregory pointed out, the world would never actually run out of commodities, they would just become prohibitively expensive the scarcer they became, so encouraging inventors and entrepreneurs to develop alternatives. Having doomsday clocks for food and fuel ticking away on the internet didn't contribute to any serious discussion about how to address the coming squeeze on resources. It didn't show any insight into what policies were needed to avoid a doomsday situation.

But despite Gregory's protests, the clocks had been a big hit. Online discussion forums and bloggers, even mainstream newspapers, were now quoting the Foundation's estimates of the diminishing amount of time that remained until the world ran out of key raw materials. Mr Steddon had been pleased with the impact, praising the combination of Gregory's analytical skills and Julian's marketing savvy.

As if to add insult to injury, Julian had created a screensaver that showed the clocks ticking down and had arranged for it to be installed on all the office's computers. According to Julian, the screensaver had been downloaded by a further 23,000 of the general public in just the past six weeks.

Gregory watched the clock on his own screen ticking down, second by second, and felt resentful and embarrassed. He'd been at the Foundation for three years now. He'd built the team from nothing, a team of bright people, passionate people, who cared for the future of the human race. And yet, somehow, Julian had persuaded most of them to his way of thinking. He'd got them all talking about the importance of influencing public opinion. Gregory felt his team deserved more. These clocks were an insult to their intelligence.

A knock on the door disturbed Gregory's thoughts. He

looked up to see his secretary, Becky, peering through the glass. He waved her in.

"The latest publicity reports just arrived from the agency," she said, placing a file on his desk. She looked excited.

"Everyone still talking about us?" Gregory tried to sound positive.

"More than ever," she nodded, flashing a smile full of innocence and youth. Becky was thirty-three years old, but Gregory was always struck by the way her smile made her seem fifteen years younger.

Becky was the first person Gregory had hired after starting the Foundation. She was an idealist and genuinely concerned about the future of humanity. But what Gregory liked most about her was her smile, so full of warmth and ease and artlessness.

Gregory looked at her and soaked up the glow of her smile. Images from a familiar daydream flickered through his head. He was a celebrity lecturer and author, speaking in front of a rapt audience. She was a young idealist, sitting in the front row, transfixed by his eloquence and intellect. Afterwards, she would approach him, shyly, holding a copy of his latest book to sign. As they talked, he would be drawn to her earnest, disarming manner, and would suggest they continue their conversation over coffee, and...

"Do you need anything else?" Becky asked.

"No, thank you," Gregory's fantasy evaporated. He was married, and would never betray his wife and family. Under different circumstances, though, he wondered if she could have fallen for him.

As Becky was leaving his office, Julian appeared in the doorway and asked if he could come in. He complimented Becky on her shoes as she passed and she smiled coquettishly. Gregory frowned. She was never as playful with him. Gregory often saw Becky leaning over Julian's desk, talking quietly, then laughing and flicking her hair. Julian seemed to draw a flirtatiousness out of her.

"I've got an idea I wanted to discuss," Julian said,

slumping into the chair opposite Gregory and crossing his legs. "You guys are always telling me that the things we consume are under-priced."

"Such as?"

"Such as beef. Didn't you tell me that a prime steak should cost a hundred pounds instead of ten pounds?"

"Something like that," Gregory nodded.

"Because none of the farmers or food companies are being charged for things like pollution and all the methane that cows fart out into the environment. Or the fact that water tables are dropping to keep producing all the corn the cows eat."

"Yes," Gregory interrupted him, "the negative externalities aren't being priced in."

"But if we did have to pay for those costs, what would the real price of things be? How much would it cost to buy a hamburger? How much to buy fish and chips? How much to buy a packet of cigarettes?"

"Or a tube of hair gel?" Gregory said.

Julian smiled and ran his fingers through his hair. "Exactly. Our consumption is way out of line with what the earth can provide. If we priced everything to bring our lifestyles back onto a sustainable path, what would the world look like?"

"So what are you proposing?"

"A campaign," Julian said, "a campaign to show the real price of stuff if we want to live sustainably. We show people that they can only really afford to eat steak once a year instead of once a month."

"People won't like the conclusions."

"Of course they won't, but it would create headlines wouldn't it? It would get people talking. We could build calculators on the website so people can see how much their weekly shopping bill should really be costing. We could build an app that people can download."

"I don't know…" Gregory said, as he thought about the idea. "It's a hugely complex task."

"It doesn't have to be exact," Julian countered, "just an approximation."

"Even so."

"Stan likes the idea."

"You discussed it with Mr Steddon?" Gregory's voice grew sharper. "Before me?"

"Only briefly, we were in the lift together."

"I wish you'd come to me first. Now there'll be an expectation."

"It's only an idea, that's all."

"Seriously, it's like the tail wagging the dog. Marketing is supposed to promote the research, not dictate the direction of the research."

"Well, think it over," Julian got up. "It could be really powerful."

Gregory stood and closed the door once again. It was impossible working with Julian. He'd tried. He'd tried his best to accommodate him and his two-dimensional view of the world. He'd tried to understand what the staff saw in him and join the sense of collegiality that Julian had built with them. But he found him too vain and shallow. How such a blatant consumer as Julian could talk about living sustainably was beyond him.

Every week he wowed the staff with his latest purchase. If it wasn't a new phone it was a new pair of designer glasses. Last week, he'd bought an antique gold watch and had the whole office discussing its merits around his desk. These were senior, educated people, and Julian had somehow intrigued them sufficiently to spend fifteen minutes discussing his new watch. How could such a trinket command their attention like that?

This week, Julian had bought his hideous crocodile-skin satchel. Gregory had tried to be enthusiastic, joining the group to comment on how stylish the new briefcase looked and to admire the unusual texture of the leather. But on the inside he didn't understand the interest and admiration at all. He felt like a fraud.

Gregory picked up the publicity reports. It was undeniable that the profile of the Foundation was rising. Julian had certainly made a difference. But had he undermined the group's credibility? Had the Foundation become a Mickey Mouse publicity machine? Gregory fought back his frustration and began to input some of the figures into his monthly report for Mr Steddon. He would want to know the results of Julian's efforts.

After a while, though, he stopped and threw the publicity reports into his bin. He couldn't concentrate. It was too mindless. He picked up his phone and called an old friend who worked nearby. It was nearly 5.00pm and they arranged to meet for a beer in the Coach & Horses on Bruton Street.

Gregory didn't usually smoke, but he bought a packet of cigarettes on the way to the pub, and over the next two hours he drank four pints of Bishop's Finger ale, smoked six cigarettes and vented his exasperation. By 7.30pm he was feeling better and made his way back to the office to finish his report.

Along the way stood an Indian restaurant and Gregory stopped to order a take-out meal of chicken masala, daal, naan bread and rice. He would take it back to his desk, finish his report and get home by 10.30pm. After his earlier frustration, Gregory felt calmer. Ahead of him lay a productive evening, with the prospect of good food to lighten the chore of completing his monthly report.

Back at the Foundation, the atmosphere was quiet. All the desks were empty and cleared of papers and files and reports. Gregory knew that many of the workers simply swept all their work into their top drawer and then pulled it out again the next morning, but he didn't mind. He fetched himself two china bowls from the kitchen and poured his curry into them.

But as he was returning to his office, Gregory heard a squeal of laughter coming from one of the meeting rooms. He looked over and saw that the lights were on inside, and the door was shut. He walked over to the room and peered through the glass window. Inside, he saw Julian and his secretary Becky. The two of them were standing in a tight embrace, Becky with her head buried in Julian's chest, and he running his fingers through her hair.

Gregory leapt back out of view. Julian had seduced his secretary, his sweet, kind, idealistic Becky. She had come under the thrall of a peacock, a vacuous dandy with the intelligence of a turnip and the principles of a mercenary. Julian didn't care for the cause of the Foundation, he was just an advertising man, a used-car salesman selling worthless platitudes.

Gregory walked back through the rows of desks and felt his anger rising with each step. How dare he? How dare he betray his position so blatantly? How dare he take advantage of an innocent girl?

The events that followed took place in a blur. When he looked back, Gregory couldn't recall what made him act as he did. His memories of that evening felt like they belonged to someone else, as if he was watching a film. Gregory could only think it was the four beers in the pub that fuelled his simmering frustration, like petrol poured on smoldering coals. But even so, he had no excuse.

Julian's desk was at one end of the open-plan area and as Gregory stared at it through his beery anger, he perceived it as an altar to the man's preening shallowness. On its surface lay a hairbrush and a tube of skin cream. And besides these, lay Julian's gold watch and his new briefcase—that nasty, vainglorious briefcase with its showy crocodile leather.

Gregory strode over to the desk and picked up the briefcase. In his anger he wanted to slash it with a knife. He thought about cutting the leather into the shape of a crocodile. Something, anything to vent his frustration. In the end, Gregory did something just as foolish. He unbuckled the flap of the briefcase, flipped it open, and poured his chicken masala inside, before rebuckling it shut.

Behind him he heard another peal of laughter and the sound of the meeting room door opening. Gregory turned round and saw Julian and Becky walking out, he with his arm resting casually on her shoulder.

"Hello Gregory," Julian said, letting his arm fall away.

"What the hell are you doing?" Gregory shouted back.

"What do you mean?"

"You know what I mean, you and Becky in the meeting room."

"We weren't doing anything."

"Like hell you weren't, I saw the two of you in each other arms."

"It was nothing."

"Don't lie! I saw you. You're bloody having an affair with my secretary," Gregory's voice was choking with anger. How dare Julian lie to him, and in that guiltless tone of voice. Without thinking, Gregory picked up Julian's hairbrush from the desk and hurled it across the office.

"What the fuck are you doing?" Julian screamed, ducking involuntarily as the brush clattered off the wall.

"What the fuck am I doing? Me?" Gregory reached down to the desk again, and this time his fingers grabbed Julian's watch. Throwing the hairbrush had released something inside him. It felt good to be angry. He grasped the watch by the leather strap and hurled it after the hairbrush.

"Will you bloody calm…" Julian shouted, but stopped as the watch flew past him.

The arc of its flight etched itself in Gregory's memory like a slow-motion replay. The action had been involuntary, an impulse response to his anger. He hadn't aimed the watch at anything, he hadn't even checked to see where it might land. But as the three of them looked on, the watch flew directly through an open window and into the four-story void above the street outside.

"Are you completely fucking insane?" Julian screamed. "That watch cost a fortune."

"I don't bloody care how much it cost. You're having an affair in my office…"

"I'm not having an affair, you idiot."

"I caught you!" Gregory screamed in return, "you're having an affair with my bloody secretary…"

"Not that it's any of your business, but…" Julian shouted, before pausing and lowering his voice, "look, Gregory, I'm gay."

"What?"

"Fucking gay… I'm homosexual, okay?"

Gregory stood blinking, lost for words. "But I saw you just now in the meeting room…"

"Becky was consoling me," Julian explained. "I had a personal issue. I wanted her advice."

"It's true," Becky said, her face looking like she might cry.

"Boyfriend trouble," Julian added, "my boyfriend, not hers."

"I'm sorry," Gregory mumbled, "I didn't know."

"What the hell's got into you?" Julian walked over to the window and looked down at the street.

"It was an error of judgement, I'm sorry," Gregory pulled himself together.

"What about my watch?"

"Tell me what type it was and I'll get you a new one."

"It was an antique, a Breitling from 1946, you won't find another like it easily."

"Then tell me what it cost and I'll give you the money. I really am sorry."

"Four thousand pounds."

"Four thousand?"

"If you go down, you might find it on the street," Becky suggested.

"Maybe," Julian said, "but it won't have survived the fall. It'll be totally smashed up."

"I really am sorry," Gregory said, "I don't know what came over me. It must be stress I think."

"Don't worry," Julian said, picking up his hairbrush. "I'll go down and see if I can find what's left of it. Maybe I can sell the gold for scrap." He returned to his desk and threw the brush into a drawer.

"There's something else I have to tell you," Gregory said, eyeing the briefcase on the desk in front of Julian with its hidden content of chicken masala. His anger had cooled into embarrassment and regret. It was he who had acted poorly. But before he could say anything more, Julian reached under his desk and pulled out an identical satchel to the one that lay on the top.

"What is it?" Julian said, straightening and tucking the case under his arm. "What did you want to say?"

"You have two briefcases?" Gregory asked, confused. "Two cases exactly the same?"

Julian shot a glance over at Becky, and then back at Gregory. "No. This one's mine," he tapped the satchel under his arm. "That one… that's a present for you."

"For me?"

"For your birthday tomorrow," Becky explained. "We all heard you admiring Julian's case, so we got you an identical one. It was supposed to be a surprise."

"Do try and act surprised when we give it you," Julian added, striding towards the door. "I'm going to look for that watch."

"I was about to wrap up the briefcase, but Julian wanted to talk," Becky said, her face still full of concern. "I didn't think you were coming back, otherwise I'd have kept it hidden."

Becky paused and sniffed the air. "What's that smell?" She spotted the China bowls that Gregory had put down on Julian's desk and walked over to inspect them. "You got take-away curry? You should have said. I'd have ordered some with you."

6

JUNE: THE REUNION

As the train clattered through the suburbs of South London on its way to Waterloo station, Liz Young watched the cityscape roll past, always more ugly and depressing when viewed from the railway than from the streets. She realised it had been more than a year since she'd last visited London. She didn't miss it.

During her twenties, the city's bars and restaurants had consumed her with a sense of possibility. The museums and galleries and theatres had offered learning and stimulation. The streets and markets had heaved with people from all over the world.

Liz had met her husband James in London. They'd bought their first apartment in South Kensington, and she'd given birth to both of their sons in the Chelsea and Westminster Hospital on Fulham Road. Her memories of London were deeply treasured. But by her early thirties, with two small children, the allure of the city had started to wane. She and James had moved out to Brockenhurst on the south coast, two hours away.

Now in her mid-forties, Liz rarely returned to the capital. James still worked there and commuted three days a week. But she preferred her life out in the country with its more modest tempo, with her garden, her local friends and community, her horse riding and the boys' sailing club. She realised now that London had always felt transient and temporary to her. By contrast, her village outside Brockenhurst felt grounded and rooted.

"You know Hibiscus has two Michelin stars?" James said. Her husband sat facing her on the train. He always commuted later than most, arriving in London around 11.00am. "It's one of the best restaurants in London."

"Yes," Liz said, peeling her gaze away from the graffiti outside. "If it was up to me, I'd have chosen somewhere a bit cheaper. I mean, I haven't seen her since I was eighteen."

"Don't worry about the cost, just enjoy the food."

"Can you believe it's twenty-seven years since I left school?"

"Twenty-nine for me…"

"But why pick such a fancy place? I can barely remember her," Liz turned back to look at the view outside the window. Despite its ugliness, the railway had a strange magnetism. "I probably won't even recognise her."

"Course you will," James said. "You were her best friend at school."

"That's not saying much. She didn't have any friends, not really. I was just kind to her."

"You obviously made an impression."

"I felt sorry for her."

"How come?"

"Being all alone like that. Can you imagine the culture shock? A thirteen-year-old Chinese girl, plucked from her home and sent to England, to St Mary's?"

"It's one of the best girls' schools in the country."

"For an English girl, maybe. Not for someone from Hong Kong."

The train was slowing now as it approached the station and passengers were already lining up at the doors.

"How did she find you anyway?" James asked.

"The school has an alumni network."

"She's living in London now?"

"That's what she said in her email. Been there two years."

"Married?"

"Yes," Liz nodded, "with two children."

"You'll have loads to talk about."

Liz frowned. "Don't you hate reunions though? They're so competitive. Everyone wants to know who made the most of their career? Whose children are doing the best? Who married the most successful husband?"

"You did," James said, "no contest there."

"Yes," Liz said, her frown softening for a moment. "But reunions always feel like a judgement, don't you think? It's all about how well you've done compared to your peers?"

"You're happy aren't you?"

"Of course I am, but still…"

"Don't worry about it," James said, standing and putting on his suit jacket. "Just enjoy yourself."

Liz reached the restaurant on Maddox Street, just behind Hanover Square, with half an hour to spare. She made her way onto New Bond Street and walked up and down the shops to kill time, occasionally entering one, but paying little attention. She felt anxious. What was she doing? Until a week ago, she hadn't given a single thought to Stella or what had become of her.

At midday, she returned to Hibiscus and pushed through the door. Inside, the restaurant was empty, save for a lone diner sitting at a table at the far end. Liz blinked to clear her eyes and stepped closer. The diner was a woman, dressed in a tight white dress. She had long black hair held back by a pair of sunglasses resting on her head. As Liz approached, the woman turned, and smiled.

"Hello," she said, rising gracefully to her feet and extending her arms. Liz smiled back and returned her embrace.

"I can't believe it's you, after all these years," Liz gushed, pulling away again and looking at Stella. "You look so different, so glamorous."

"Not a shy school girl any more."

"Hardly, you look like a model."

It was true. Stella seemed to have grown several inches taller and looked slim and groomed. Her skin was flawless, as smooth as jade, and her eyes were cool and dark—far more knowing than the innocent eighteen-year-old that Liz had once known.

"You look well too," Stella said, gesturing for Liz to sit.

"Nonsense," Liz laughed, pulling out her chair. She felt dowdy and middle-aged opposite Stella. "If I didn't know otherwise, I'd say you were thirty."

"Too much pampering," Stella said, pulling an expression of mock disapproval, "too much time on my hands."

"Don't complain, you look amazing. So what are you doing here, in London I mean? What brought you back to England?"

"My husband, Richard."

"He's English is he?"

"No, from Hong Kong. He's with Bank of North Asia. We got posted here two years ago."

"He works in the City?"

"Every hour that god sends," Stella rolled her eyes. "That's his real wife, his job. I'm just a mistress."

"When did you get married?"

"1998… fourteen years ago."

"James and I are coming up for nineteen years this summer."

"You got married young…"

"I was twenty-six. It didn't feel young at the time."

"And still happy?"

"Yes," Liz nodded. "We have two great children, two sons, and James is a great dad. He's kind to me…"

"What about the sex?"

"The sex?" Liz said, taken aback at the question.

"You still enjoy sex with him?"

"I, I… yes, of course."

"Good," Stella said, picking up the menu in front of her.

"Your husband sounds more attentive than mine. Shall we order drinks? How about a glass of champagne?"

"Lovely," Liz said, trying to sound enthusiastic. In truth, she felt unnerved. Stella wasn't at all what she'd expected. Not only glamorous, but forthright, and confident—a world away from the quiet girl at school who had lived in the library.

"Have you eaten here before?" Stella asked. "The crab and mango salad's good. The pollock was also good last time I came."

A waiter took their orders and other diners began to arrive which put Liz more at ease. "Tell me more about you," she said. "Tell me about the kids."

"I have two girls," Stella said. "Grace is twelve and Pearl is nine."

"I love their names," Liz smiled, "they sound so British, Victorian even."

"They have Chinese ones too, but we don't use them here."

"I suppose that makes it easier to fit in."

"Maybe. Children are so adaptable, though, don't you find?"

"Really?"

"Yeah. The girls have settled in so well. Their school's great, they've made some good friends."

"I'm delighted. And you've settled in too?"

"Yes, well, sort of… it wasn't easy at first."

"No?"

"It helps if you have a job. Otherwise it's hard to meet people."

"I'm sure that's true."

"Richard was quite against the idea, though. He prefers me to be a wife and a mother."

"Sounds old-fashioned…"

"He is a bit, although it's not like we need the money. He does very well."

"I can't imagine how you'd work anyway, what with looking after your girls."

"Oh, that wouldn't be an issue," Stella waved her hand dismissively. "We have two maids, two Filipino girls, who live with us."

"In your home?"

Stella nodded and sipped her champagne. "We brought them over with us from Hong Kong."

"What do they do, these two girls?"

"Anything. Cleaning, cooking, washing. They get Grace and Pearl ready for school in the morning, cook their meals. They do the shopping most weeks."

"What a luxury."

"It's quite normal in Hong Kong…"

"Not in England," Liz paused. "So… if you don't work, and you have all that help, what do you do with your time?"

"Like I said, lots of pampering."

"How amazing."

"You'd think so, wouldn't you? But I went through a phase of being very bored and lonely. It's not easy to meet people in London."

"What about the girls' school, the other mums, you must have met some of them…"

"They're alright, but they already have close friends," Stella shrugged. "I tried other things too, oil painting and cooking classes, but after a while it all feels a bit pointless. You get tired of it."

"I suppose…" Liz said, not completely convinced.

"Actually I got quite depressed," Stella continued. "Richard was always at work, or out with clients. I didn't have any family or anyone to spend time with, the girls were at school. The first year went very slowly." Stella paused, "It's interesting, isn't it? When you're bored and unhappy, life moves at its slowest. But when you're really enjoying yourself, it speeds by."

"Yes," Liz agreed, "it should be the other way round, shouldn't it?"

"Anyway, things are much better now."

A waiter arrived carrying their starters and placed them on

the table. Liz watched as he fussed over the table setting and filled their water glasses.

"What happened?" She asked when he was gone. "What changed to make your second year so much better?"

"I don't know if..." Stella hesitated, staring at Liz, her expression now more serious than earlier. "I've never told anyone before."

"It's okay," Liz said. "I wasn't trying to be nosy."

"I would like to tell you," Stella said, and then smiled. "At school, I always felt I could trust you. But you mustn't think badly of me."

"It's not something illegal is it?"

"No," Stella laughed.

"Then I won't think badly of you. What was it?"

"I discovered a book."

"A book?" Liz wondered if Stella had found god.

"It's called *Fear of Flying*. Have you read it? By a writer called Erica Jong."

"Isn't it some sort of feminist manifesto?"

"Not really, it's a novel. Although, it does encourage women to take hold of their lives."

"I remember people talking about it," Liz said, "but years ago."

"Yeah, it was published in the seventies."

"So it changed your life, this book? What's in it?"

"It's about a woman locked in a stale marriage," Stella said. "Isadora Wing. She's 29, she's been married for five years, and already she sees her life as flat and dull, you know, an eternity of exactly the same stretching ahead of her."

"Tedium..."

"Exactly. Hold on a minute," Stella reached for her handbag. "I have a copy of it here. It's always with me."

She unzipped the bag and began emptying the contents onto the table in front of her: a purse, sunglasses case, make-up, mobile phone, a gold watch, and finally she extracted the book.

Liz watched her, wondering what could be in the book

that had influenced her so deeply. But when she saw the gold watch, her attention shifted. She recognised it.

"That's a rather male looking watch," she said, mostly as an excuse so that she could pick it up and inspect it.

Three weeks earlier, her eldest son, Nathan, had been on a school trip to London. A group of students had travelled up to the city to attend a science lecture and exhibition at the Royal Institution. After it had finished, Nathan and his friends had been walking down to Green Park tube station on their way home when Nathan had felt something land in the hood of his coat.

At first, he'd assumed one of his friends had thrown something at him. But after retrieving the missile from his hood, he discovered it was a gold watch. None of his group had seen it land, nor could they see who might have thrown it. The street had still been light with the summer evening, but whoever had dispatched the watch was either in hiding or had disappeared.

Nathan had told his parents, Liz and James, about the incident, but neither of them could understand why somebody would have thrown away such a valuable watch in such a strange way. Nathan had suggested it was a passing vehicle, and that whoever had hurled the watch from the car had done so intentionally, otherwise they would surely have stopped to reclaim it. For her part, Liz wondered if the watch had been stolen and somebody was trying to get rid of it. Possibly it was incriminating evidence of some kind, the link to a murder.

Liz had felt uncomfortable about keeping the watch, not knowing its provenance, but Nathan had declared his intention to wear it. He liked the mystery. And it was a handsome watch—old and well worn, but attractive, and with a curious inscription on the back: "May your brief candle shine brightly." Nathan had identified with that too.

As Liz picked up the watch from the table, she felt a tremor of fear. The watch looked identical to the one that Nathan had found. She knew it was irrational to think that Stella, a long-lost school friend, might now have the self same watch in her handbag, but something in her sub-conscious urged her to check.

"Here," Stella said, leafing through the book, "I've underlined some of the text. Let me read you this bit, it's Isadora, the main character, talking about her marriage: 'Even if you loved your husband, there came that inevitable year when fucking him turned as bland as Velveeta cheese: filling, fattening even, but no thrill to the tastebuds, no bittersweet edge, no danger'." Stella looked up. "That's exactly how I felt with Richard."

Liz turned over the watch in her hand. There, on the underside, was the same inscription as the one on her son's watch. Liz stared at it blankly. The chance of two antique watches, of identical kinds, having identical inscriptions was impossibly remote. This was surely the same watch that Nathan had been wearing up until... Liz didn't know. She had assumed her son was still wearing it.

"Do you see?" Stella continued. "Marriages go stale. And women get trapped in these stale relationships, all the spark in their lives extinguished. That was me. Stuck here in London, with no friends, and no purpose, and a husband who... well, there was nothing between us, no thrill."

"I'm sorry to hear that," Liz said. She dearly wanted to ask Stella about the watch, but without drawing undue attention to it.

"But the thing is, the book also showed me a way out of the trap."

"Not an affair?" Liz said, looking up from the table.

"Not in the traditional sense," Stella said, her eyes wide with excitement. "In the book, Isadora does have an affair. But she explores some of her other fantasies too. The purest of them all is the 'Zipless fuck'."

"The Zipless..." Liz shied away from completing the phrase. The word was so harsh, so brutal.

"The Zipless fuck," Stella repeated the phrase. "It's a fantasy where two strangers meet and have sex with each other. No emotional involvement, no personal histories, no relationship complications, no baggage at all. Just pure physical sex. Neither the man nor the woman know a thing about the other. They make love and never see each other again."

"That's not what you're doing? Is it?" Liz asked. "You're not having sex with strangers are you?"

"You can't believe how exhilarating it is."

"You have sex with men you've never met before?" Liz looked down at the watch and felt her stomach turn.

"Complete strangers," Stella nodded. "Honestly, you wouldn't believe how it makes you feel. The first time I asked a man I was nearly sick with nerves. I was in Harvey Nicholls… the department store? I'd been thinking about the Zipless Fuck for weeks, and then I noticed this man who was staring at me. He was in his late twenties, maybe early thirties, tall, slim, short hair. He looked handsome and well-dressed, and I realised he was watching me."

"What did you do?"

"I went up to him. He was German, by the way. At least his accent sounded German. Honestly, my heart was pounding like a jackhammer. Can you imagine the feeling of danger, the potential for humiliation, for something to go wrong… Anyway, I gave it a try."

"What did you say?"

"I said I'd noticed him staring at me. He was a bit embarrassed, but I just came out with it. I asked him if he wanted to have sex with me."

"You didn't…"

"Can you believe it?" Stella beamed. "Just like that. And he said yes."

"Where?"

"In one of the changing rooms."

"Just out of nowhere, you propositioned this man and then had sex with him?"

"Honestly, it was as simple as that."

"Did you use protection?" Liz asked.

"I had condoms with me."

"What… How was it?"

"Unbelievable. I don't know if the sex was anything special, probably just okay. But the thrill of it, the danger, the excitement. I never knew his name. He never knew my name."

"No conversation?"

"Not really. Afterwards, I just left him there. I walked away and never looked back."

"And you've done it with other men too?"

"Yeah, quite a few…"

"I can't believe it," Liz said, shocked and unsure how to respond. "And you actually enjoy it?"

"Nothing makes you feel so alive," Stella beamed. "Every time you do it, you put yourself in a position of… I don't know, incredible vulnerability, but also incredible power. There's always the worry that something might go wrong, but the adrenaline rush, and the feeling afterwards, like you've made a conquest. You've broken a taboo, experienced something completely primitive and powerful. It feels like… like animals on the savannah, you know? Pursuing our basest urge, but stripped of all its social convention."

"It could be so dangerous. It could really go badly if you approach the wrong person," Liz said.

"I'm careful who I choose. They have to be clean, good-looking, nice clothes. And I choose places that are safe—museums, libraries, department stores, places where there are lots of other people. That adds to the excitement, you know. Doing it with so many other people around, and none of them aware of what's happening."

The waiter cleared away their plates and served them with their entrees. The gold watch was still sitting on the table and Liz wondered how she could ask Stella about it. She had grown nervous as the conversation had progressed. She didn't feel like eating.

"Is this Richard's watch?" she asked awkwardly as Stella repacked her handbag.

"God, no," Stella said, taking it from Liz's hand and dropping it into her bag. "He wouldn't wear something so old. Everything has to be the very latest thing with him. Strange isn't it?"

"What is?"

"That he's so old-fashioned, but everything he owns is so modern."

"So whose watch is it?" Liz persisted.

"I don't know," Stella shrugged. And began to eat her fish. "It belongs to a guy I met."

"One of your conquests?" Liz asked, her tone a little sharper than she had intended.

"Now you're judging me," Stella said. "You promised you wouldn't."

"Sorry, I'm just intrigued."

"He was some guy I met on a train. Richard had a client thing happening in Southampton last week and he wanted me to go with him. Wives were required for that one. There was a dinner and, honestly, it was so dull! I left the next morning but Richard stayed on. So I was on the train coming back to London on my own and saw this guy sitting across from me. We made eye contact, and one thing led to another."

"On the train?"

"Yeah."

"Where?"

"In one of the bathrooms. The watch must have fallen off his wrist. I meant to hand it in to the Lost & Found at the station, but completely forgot."

"No, I meant where was the train when you met this guy?"

"Where was the train? No idea. Somewhere outside Southampton."

Liz felt her stomach tighten further. She couldn't eat at all now. Nathan's school term had finished ten days earlier and he was spending the summer working in Winchester, one of the stops on the Southampton to London line. Liz had a friend restoring an old house there, and Nathan had been invited to join the team as a labourer for a holiday job. He was taking the train every day from their home in Brockenhurst, going through Southampton, and then on to Winchester.

"Last week, you say?" Liz asked.

"Yes," Stella nodded. "It wasn't the best liaison I've ever had. He was rather desperate, a bit fumbly. It was all over very quickly."

Was it any surprise, Liz thought. Nathan was only seventeen. It would have been his first time. To lose his virginity like that. It was horrible.

"Will you excuse me for a minute," Liz said, stumbling to her feet. "I'm just going to the bathroom."

"Are you okay?" Stella asked. "The bathroom's over there."

Liz locked the door behind her and sank to her knees. She wanted to vomit, but couldn't. Poor Nathan, she kept saying to herself. Her innocent son, her first-born, a victim of this woman's trap. Images of Nathan and Stella having sex on the train swirled through her head. Grim bathroom fittings, graffiti scratched into the plastic walls, Nathan's trousers on the floor, soaking up puddles of urine around the toilet bowl. And Stella touching him, touching her son, kissing him, holding his penis, fucking him. How could he do it? How could Nathan give himself away so cheaply? She felt angry and cheated—even jealous that Stella had experienced a closeness with her son that she never could.

Back at the table, Liz found she could no longer look Stella in the eye. The situation was too uncomfortable. Instead, she complained that she was feeling too sick to carry on. A stomach bug, she said. She needed to leave.

Stella was full of concern and offered to take her to hospital, or to her house, which was twenty minutes away in Regent's Park. Liz could lie down and recover, she suggested. But Liz insisted she would simply go home. She apologised, and promised that they would meet again soon and catch up properly.

Liz caught a taxi to Waterloo Station, and from there took the train home. It was 4.30pm by the time she walked through her front door. The house was empty. Her youngest son was sailing, and Nathan wouldn't be back from his renovation project in Winchester until after 6.00pm.

During the train journey, her thoughts had calmed considerably. The further she travelled from London, the more she persuaded herself that there must be an alternative explanation. It was simply too incredible that a school friend who she hadn't seen for twenty-seven years had taken her son's virginity. And that she had done so on a train, of all places, and just one week before their reunion. There must be another explanation.

Liz changed into her jeans and pulled the lawnmower from the garage. The grass in front of the house needed cutting and it was a pleasant evening. She would mow the lawn and get to the bottom of things when Nathan returned.

By the time she saw him walking down the lane towards their house from the bus stop, the grass was cut, she'd watered the hanging baskets, weeded a flowerbed and raked the gravel in the drive. She felt on top of the garden, and watched with pleasure as Nathan strode towards her.

It was nearly seven o'clock, and his blond hair looked golden in the softening sunlight. How handsome he was, she thought. A boy who was now almost a man, tall, and with shoulders that stretched his shirt.

"Hello darling," she said, giving him a hug. Nathan returned the embrace half-heartedly.

"What's up mum?"

"Nothing, just pleased to see you," Liz pulled back and looked at her son. His wrists were covered with the sleeves of his shirt. "Do you still have that watch you found?"

"Sure," he nodded.

"You're wearing it?"

"No."

"Why not?"

"I didn't want to wear it while we're fixing up the house."

"Why?"

"I thought it'd get scratched."

"So you left it here? At home?"

"Why are you so interested in the watch?"

"Just answer me Nathan. Is it here?"

"No, I gave it to Dad to look after," he said. "I took the train with him the other morning and forgot I was wearing it. When I got off at Winchester, I asked him to look after it."

"So Dad's got it now?"

"Yeah, but it's in London."

"How do you know?"

"I asked him for it yesterday, and he didn't have it on him. He said he'd left it at his office."

7

JULY: DOING TIME

Josie Linggo stared at her reflection in the mirror where one side of her face was lit up with gold. Outside, the sun was intense and bright and made the morning dance with expectation. Summer streamed in through the bathroom windows, and the warmth and light made Josie feel almost as if she were in her native Philippines.

She studied her reflection, admiring the wrinkle-free curves of her face and the gloss of her long black ponytail. She puffed out her chest and felt happy. Her new top showed off her breasts in just the right way. She was sure Amado would approve.

Josie picked up her digital camera and aimed it at the mirror, taking a number of pictures from a variety of angles. She looked through them, then took several more pictures until she was satisfied she had captured the look she wanted. She would send them to Amado later that day.

Outside the bathroom, the house was quiet. Ma'am Stella and her husband and two daughters had already left for the day. And Maricelle was doing the weekly shopping as she did every Saturday. Josie wandered into the kitchen and padded up and down, watching birds hopping across the lawn outside. Tending the garden was one of her jobs, and she was proud of her work. Being a London garden, it was only small, but the plants were glorious and healthy, an opulence of different greens and the irrepressible blossoms of blue and white hydrangeas.

Josie glanced at the kitchen clock. It was 11.00am. Maricelle was late as usual. Josie felt sure she did the shopping on Saturdays to annoy her. And that she took as long as possible. Saturdays were Josie's day off, but she couldn't leave until Maricelle had returned from the supermarket.

She walked over to the white board next to the fridge where Ma'am Stella wrote down the items that Maricelle needed to buy. Her handwriting was a stream of circles and loops that barely changed from one letter to another, making her words look like stretched springs. Josie rubbed out the bottom entry on the list, picked up the marker pen and re-wrote the entry in near perfect mimicry. It was her one form of revenge on Maricelle—adding unnecessary items to the shopping list that Ma'am Stella would question, or else adding heavy items that Maricelle would struggle to carry back.

Josie sauntered out of the kitchen and through the hallway into the drawing room at the front of the house. From the window she could watch the road. She leant on the back of the sofa and waited. At least she would have the next four weeks to herself. Maricelle was leaving the following day for her annual holiday to the Philippines.

It was 11.30am by the time Maricelle struggled down the street laden with bags. Josie was tempted to go out and help her in order to hasten the start of her day-off, but the sight of Maricelle puffing and panting was too pleasing to disturb.

"You're not going out in that are you?" Maricelle asked when she pushed through the front door and deposited the shopping in the hall. "You look like a Manila bar-girl."

Josie smiled and helped her carry the bags through to the kitchen. It was too nice a day to rise to the bait. And anyway, she had the prospect of the next four weeks to herself.

It meant more work for Josie. As well as her duties cleaning the house and doing the washing and ironing and the gardening, she would also have to look after the two girls, walk them to school in the morning, pick them up in the afternoon, cook their meals and oversee their bathtime. But she didn't mind the extra work. At least Maricelle would be out of her hair. No snide comments about the quality of her cleaning. No put-downs about her being lazy. No criticism of her appearance. And best of all, she'd have her room to herself.

Once the shopping was unpacked, Josie picked up her bag and skipped out into the sunshine. She didn't know many people in London, and those she did know—other Filipina domestic workers—had Sunday as their day off. Josie had tried to negotiate with Maricelle to alternate their days off so that Josie could meet up with her friends every now and then, but Maricelle had refused to swap even one of her Sundays.

And so Josie spent her days off alone, usually in an internet café behind Oxford Street, or else browsing the shops. Occasionally she saw a film in Leicester Square, or went down to the Filipino centre in Hammersmith to catch up on gossip from home. But her time in the internet café was always the most precious. It was there that she connected with Amado. Settling into her usual spot by the window, Josie opened her email account and saw several new messages.

Amado worked as a lorry driver in Saudi Arabia. Like Josie, he was one of ten million Filipinos who worked outside the shores of their homeland, a vast army of economic refugees fleeing the corruption and incompetence of their native government. He was 26, the same age as Josie, and every week he sent her an email without fail.

His message this week was typical. He spoke of the harsh work driving trucks through the Arabian heat—often without air-conditioning—and described the journeys he'd made and the goods he'd delivered. He complained of the boredom of his days off, with nothing to do and nowhere to go but the barrack hut in his camp in the desert outside Damman. The men cooked food and played football on an area of hardened sand once the sun had cooled in the late afternoon. The barracks had a TV, although nothing worth watching on it, and an old computer that just about managed to send emails.

But despite the hardships, Amado contented himself with thoughts of Josie and how they would be married one day. He and Josie had met three years earlier in their home town of Batangas City. Both of them had been working overseas—Josie for Ma'am Stella in Hong Kong, before moving to London. Every year, Josie and Amado timed their annual trip home so that they could see each other again. On their last trip, Amado had proposed. Since first meeting him, Josie had spent exactly 31 days in his company, but she knew that she loved him.

Amado was a romantic, a poet at heart. He loved to sing and had a voice that Josie believed was the very embodiment of the Philippine islands, with their breezes and verdance and lapping seas. He called her Sampaguita, a fragrant white flower from the jasmine family that filled the evenings at home with rich perfume.

One day they would be married, he promised. He just needed to save enough money for them to be together. It wasn't easy. Every month, it seemed, his employers in Saudi found some reason to deduct the wages they paid. Drivers had to pay their own traffic fines, and were punished if their delivery arrived later than scheduled. Often the drivers' wages were cut for no good reason at all. Amado was supposed to receive 1,600 Saudi riyals a month, but sometimes it dropped to just 1,000—roughly 170 pounds.

Josie earned more than Amado, and saved her money diligently. But she had her own problems too. With her mother ill and her father unemployed, it was up to Josie to support them. Every month, she visited the Western Union office and wired two thirds of her salary back to the Philippines to support them. She had an elder brother who worked as a seaman in Malaysia, but he had his own family to support, and so the burden of looking after her parents fell largely on Josie's shoulders. Sometimes she wondered if she and Amado would ever save enough to settle down.

Josie read and re-read the email, and then replied with her own news, attaching the best of the photos that she had taken that morning to her email. The other two emails were from her sister-in-law in the Philippines and from a friend in Hong Kong, another domestic helper who had worked in the same apartment block as her. Josie replied to them too, and then made her way to a Filipino restaurant on Edgware Road. She ate adobo chicken and rice, and bought a piece of panutsa—peanuts set in toffee—to take home and have that evening. Several of the other tables had Filipinos sitting in groups and Josie enjoyed hearing her native Tagalog being spoken so abundantly, albeit with variations on her own dialect.

That afternoon, she visited Selfridges department store, and admired the dresses by Alexander McQueen and Stella McCartney. She could never hope to buy one, but she enjoyed their elegance and seeing them displayed with such glamour.

Later, she walked in Hyde Park, and watched the boats on the Serpentine and the rollerbladers screaming up and down the path that ran parallel to Park Lane where they slalomed round piles of jumpers and bags and water bottles. At Speakers' Corner, Josie stopped for a minute to listen to a man standing on a stepladder clutching a black bible.

"And as St Peter wrote in his First Epistle," the preacher shouted, catching Josie's eye. "People are like grass, and all their glories are like the flowers of the field; but the grass withers and the flowers wilt and fall."

Josie shivered and hurried away, filled with a sense of her own mortality. She was in her time of blossom, Amado too. Were they destined to spend their brief moment of glory apart? Everywhere Josie looked, she saw couples walking hand-in-hand, and Josie dreamt that one day she and Amado might do the same, laying out a rug under one of the plane trees and playing guitar.

It was 8.15pm by the time she returned to the house in Regent's Park. Ma'am Stella and her husband were leaving for a dinner party as she climbed the steps to the front door, and inside Maricelle was putting the girls to bed. Josie went up to her room, flicked on the television and lay down on her bed. Maricelle's side of the room was a chaos of clothes and shoes and an open suitcase that was half-packed for her flight to Manila the next morning. Josie surveyed the mess to make sure that Maricelle hadn't packed anything of hers. Maricelle was older than Josie, and plumper, but it was worth checking. All seemed in order, and Josie dozed on her bed as the television droned in the background.

Some time later, she was woken by the sound of Maricelle bustling next to her. Josie opened her eyes and watched her absently.

"What time is your flight?" she asked, shifting onto her side.

The question startled Maricelle and she threw what she was holding into the suitcase and flicked the lid shut. "10.00am," she said, turning to face Josie.

"So you have to leave the house around 7.30?" Josie replied. She sat up on the edge of her bed and tried to see what it was that Maricelle had been so keen to hide.

"Probably a bit earlier," Maricelle said. She turned back to her bag, zipped it shut and put it on the floor next to her bed.

Josie stared at the bag. It was small—small enough to take on as hand luggage—but Maricelle still had things on her bed that needed packing. Had she zipped it up because she had run out of space? Or was she trying to hide something? Josie felt sure it was the latter. But what? Had she taken something of Josie's while she was asleep?

Josie remembered her piece of panutsa and went down to the kitchen to make a cup of tea and eat her peanut brittle. From upstairs came the faint sound of Maricelle lumbering around and opening and shutting the wardrobe in her room. And then came the familiar creaks of her walking to the bathroom and closing the door. Josie crept out into the hall and heard the shower start to run. Now was her chance.

She tiptoed back up the two flights of stairs, walking close to the walls to avoid the floorboards that would betray her passage. Back in her bedroom, she tugged Maricelle's suitcase onto the bed and unzipped it. On top were clothes, neatly folded, and beneath them lay t-shirts as gifts for her nephews, and shoes and a packet of photos and postcards of London that Maricelle had collected to show her friends at home. At the bottom of the case, Josie found a brown cardboard box the size and shape of a paperback book. She took it out and pulled off the lid.

As she did so, the bathroom door opened and Josie heard footsteps returning to the bedroom. She turned to look at Maricelle, her face full of shock and fear.

"What are you doing?' Maricelle asked. "You went through my bag?"

"I thought you'd packed some of my clothes," Josie stammered, "by mistake. I was just checking."

"You have no right," Maricelle shouted, then lowered her voice. "You have no right…"

"But what's this?" Josie asked. "This isn't yours."

"It's none of your business," Maricelle grabbed the box and tried to force the lid back on again.

"That belongs to Ma'am Stella." The box was packed with jewellery. There was a thick gold rope that Josie recognised instantly as one that Ma'am Stella wore regularly, and another necklace with a rich pendant of rubies. Josie had seen diamond earrings, a gold charm bracelet, a man's gold watch and other items too.

"It's nothing to do with you," Maricelle threw the box back into her suitcase and zipped it shut once more.

"You're stealing her jewellery?"

"If you tell her, I'll kill you," Maricelle said, turning and facing Josie. "You know I will, I'll rip out your hair."

Josie sank onto her bed, and pulled her knees up to her chest. She wanted to cry. "When they find out, you won't be here. They'll blame me."

"No they won't. They'll know it was me."

"What if you get caught?"

"I won't get caught."

"You might..."

"How? Ma'am and Sir won't be back till late tonight. They'll go straight to bed. And by the time they wake up tomorrow, I'll be on a plane."

"But how will you come back?"

"I'm not coming back."

"Not coming back to England?"

"Never," Maricelle said, her eyes full of defiance. "This is my retirement. I'm 37 years old. I can't stand it any more. Looking after those spoilt girls, taking orders, living with you, living through the winters."

"They'll tell the police. They'll find you in Manila."

"They don't even know where I live." Maricelle sat down on her bed and unzipped the bag, pulling out the box in order to repack it properly. "What's it worth? Twenty thousand pounds? A bit more? It's nothing to them. We've seen sir's bank letters. He's got a hundred times that. He doesn't need it. But this buys me a house. Two houses—I can rent out one of them to lodgers. And I can set up a little restaurant and live comfortably."

"What if they think we did it together? They might get rid of me..."

"Of course they won't. How would Ma'am Stella cope with no help at all? Think about it, it's actually good for you. They'll make you the senior maid. You'll earn more money, you'll get to do the girls and the shopping."

"Who'll do the cleaning and washing?"

"They'll bring in someone else."

"They'll be so angry when they find out."

"You can worry all you like. But I warn you, if you say a word... just forget you saw anything."

"When they find out, they'll see it in my face that I knew. I can't lie to them."

"It's easy. Just act stupid. Cry—you're good at that." Maricelle closed the box properly and tucked it under her arm. "I'm going to have a shower." She got up and walked out of the bedroom, taking the box with her. She stopped at the door and pointed at Josie, "Not a word."

Josie lay down and thought about it. Perhaps Maricelle was right. Perhaps this was an opportunity for her. A better job, better pay, and she'd get Sundays off instead of Saturdays. She wished she could speak to Amado, but the camp where he was based for the moment didn't have mobile phone reception.

She went back downstairs to finish making her tea. Her panutsa was sitting on the kitchen table, but Josie didn't feel like eating. She wrapped it up and tucked it into the fridge. She had little choice, she realised. She just had to hope Ma'am Stella wouldn't blame her in any way.

Later that evening, Josie lay in bed as Maricelle watched television. Maricelle had to stay up until Ma'am Stella came home in case the girls woke up. It was nearly 1.00am when the front door opened and Josie heard voices downstairs. Maricelle got up and went down to meet them. They exchanged a few words and then all three came upstairs. Maricelle closed the door to their room, and climbed into bed.

"They might notice now," Josie whispered, "when she's taking off her jewellery."

"Shut up and go to sleep," Maricelle said.

Josie lay in silence for a long time afterwards, but no sound came from downstairs. Eventually even Maricelle was asleep and Josie lay listening to her slow, even breathing, marvelling at how she could be so calm.

The following morning, Maricelle's alarm went off at 6.30am, and the two of them got up. Josie felt tired and nervous. She hadn't slept at all, not even a minute. She needed to get up and lay the breakfast table and prepare the house for the day, but she lingered in the room, watching Maricelle get dressed and brush her hair and make her bed.

"Go on, get downstairs," Maricelle hissed at her. "Don't give them any reason to suspect anything."

"Nobody's awake yet."

"The girls will be up soon."

Josie went to the bathroom, washed her face and got

dressed. Her heart was beating with adrenaline. She was sure it showed in her face. She looked at her reflection and practiced her smile. Just act like normal, she told herself.

By 7.00am, Maricelle was down in the hallway with her bag. She drank a glass of orange juice in the kitchen, looked around the room one last time, and made her way to the front door. Josie followed her, aware that this would be the last time they saw each other. She felt oddly emotional, but Maricelle left without saying a word. She carried her bag down to the street, pulled out the handle, and walked away to the underground station, wheeling it behind her.

Moments later, the girls were downstairs too, switching on the television in the kitchen and demanding breakfast. Josie found their innocence to be calming and she set to her regular routines, pouring juice and making toast and opening the curtains and windows. Ma'am Stella didn't emerge until 8.30am when she joined her daughters in the kitchen and Josie made her a pot of tea. It wasn't until 10.00am that the theft was discovered.

Ma'am Stella was angry and shouted a lot, but it was her husband who was truly furious, ransacking Josie's room, more out of anger than in hope of finding the stolen jewellery. His daughters cowered in their own bedroom, and Josie cried genuine tears of terror and trembled with each new insult and accusation.

Ma'am Stella quickly concluded that Maricelle was responsible, and her husband called the police to report the crime and to see if her plane could be stopped and Maricelle arrested before it left. Nothing could be done, but he still went to the police station later that day to make a formal report. For Josie, that was the most terrifying part, for he dragged her along with him. The police sat her in a room for a long time and asked her what she knew about the theft. The officer was gentle and spoke with a friendly voice, but all through the interrogation Josie shook with fear and cried repeatedly.

By the evening, Josie felt drained and exhausted. She had eaten nothing all day and went to bed soon after the girls, too anxious and worn out even to change her clothes. She slept fitfully, often waking in a panic and grasping her alarm clock to check the time. At 6.00am, she got up. She couldn't sleep any more. Her stomach was still tight with nerves. She thought of Maricelle. She would have landed in Manila by now.

In fact it took Maricelle a little longer to reach her destination than planned. Her flight to Hong Kong had gone smoothly, but the last leg, from Hong Kong to Manila had been delayed by three hours. When she finally emerged from the airport into the heat of Manila, Maricelle felt tired but happy. She was home now, she thought to herself. She had worked as a domestic helper in Hong Kong for twelve years, and a further two in London. But now she was back where she belonged.

She found a stall selling drinks and bought herself a tin of coconut milk, ice cold and refreshing. She sat on a low wall with her bag on her knees as she drank it. When she had finished, she unzipped her bag and slipped her hand inside to check for the cardboard box.

It was still there, at the bottom of the case. But as she lifted it gently, the box felt strangely light. Maricelle pulled it out of her case. It felt empty. A wave of panic rushed over her and she dropped her bag to the floor as she opened the lid. Inside was a piece of paper, covered in the familiar loops and circles of Ma'am Stella's handwriting. The message was brief:

> "Maricelle—I'm very disappointed in you. Josie told us about your plan to steal my jewellery. Consider your employment terminated. You're lucky we didn't call the police—Stella."

8

AUGUST: A TIME OF PHARAOHS

Edward Tenure stepped out of his hotel in Regent's Park and made his way along the street. He'd flown into London from Geneva the day before, and had spotted a jewellery shop near the hotel on his ride in from the airport. He wanted to buy a watch. It was important that he project an image of success, and the cheap digital timepiece he usually wore was far from adequate.

Inside the shop, Edward wasn't sure what to look for. The glass cases were filled with watches of every conceivable style, from masculine diving chronometers to gaudy creations of diamonds and rubies.

"I need a watch that suggests refinement and elegance," Edward explained to the shop assistant. "It has to give the impression of wealth, but in a quiet way."

"What sort of watch?" the assistant asked. "A dress watch? A sports watch? Something to wear everyday?"

"Everyday, I suppose, but smart too."

"Do you have a budget in mind?"

"Not really." It was true—Edward could afford any watch he wanted. Two weeks earlier he had become immensely rich.

The first few pieces the assistant brought forward missed the mark. The price tags were rich, but they seemed flashy, like badges of the nouveau riche.

"Do you have something older?" Edward asked. "Something with heritage?"

"We have a collection of antique watches?" the assistant suggested.

"Show me," Edward nodded.

The assistant ushered Edward to a different part of the shop where the two of them pored over an extensive range of antiques. After half an hour, Edward picked up a gold watch, a Breitling.

"It's quite rare," the assistant said. "It was made in the 1940s, an aviator's watch. We acquired it two weeks ago. A young woman from the Philippines brought it in."

"The Philippines?"

"It's not Filipino, though. Breitling is Swiss."

"Yes," Edward nodded. "I live in Geneva. I'm familiar with the brand." He strapped it on and admired the way it looked on his wrist. The watch was stylish and spoke of sophistication and quiet confidence. "I'll take it," Edward said, pocketing his old digital timepiece and pulling out his wallet.

His next stop was Saville Row where he picked out a dinner jacket and shirt. It occurred to him that he should probably have had the suit tailored, but he didn't have time. Physically he was in good shape, so the dinner jacket fitted neatly without any need for adjustment. By midday, he had added a pair of antique silver cufflinks, a new pair of shoes and a smart leather carry-all by Mulberry to his purchases.

Edward returned to his hotel and repacked his things into the new bag. A valet brought round his Jaguar XKR and Edward slipped into the leather driver's seat. He wondered if he should have chosen a less flashy car. His old Renault back in Geneva never drew any attention, but this car was expensive and money signified success. Edward found it uncomfortable that people peered in through the windows to see his face, to see what success looked like.

It was a Friday afternoon and his destination was the Yorkshire Dales where he was spending the weekend in a country estate near Sedbergh. It belonged to Colin Lamb, an old friend of his from Cambridge University. Edward had graduated in 1997 and hadn't seen Colin since leaving Cambridge. In fact, he hadn't seen any of his old university friends since then. Fifteen years with almost no contact, and now he was driving to a reunion—a reunion of The Pharaohs.

They were in their late thirties now, a world away from the youth and gaucheness of student days. As he drove, Edward wondered how everyone would have changed. Most of all, he wondered about Amber. How would she have changed? It was on a weekend gathering of The Pharaohs, more than fifteen years earlier, that his path with Amber had changed course so sharply.

Most of the journey to Sedbergh was dull motorway, but once in the Dales, the road narrowed and fought its way through a bleak landscape of immense hills and stone walls and ruined barns. Each valley seemed to have its own weather, with driving squalls of rain and thunderous darkness in one, followed by rich sunshine and steaming hillsides in the next.

Colin's estate was tucked into a hollow half-way up the side of the Garsdale valley. The road snaked along the wooded floor of the valley, crisscrossing the narrow torrent of the Clough River. Just beyond the village of Garsdale itself, a lane lined with beech trees led off the road for half a mile up to the estate.

At the top of the lane, the coarse grass fields full of sheep and rocks gave way to sweeping lawns and cypress trees and rose beds. The main house was an imposing three-storey construction of earthy brown stone topped with slate roofs and a multitude of chimneys. A number of other buildings—stables and barns and workshops—were clustered to the side.

Edward parked on the gravel driveway next to two Range Rovers and a Mercedes and got out. The afternoon air was still warm, and the views over the valley were breathtaking. Edward's home in Geneva looked out over impressive vistas too, but this landscape was different—tougher and grittier and steeped in the hardship of generations of hill-farmers.

"Eddy? Is that you?" Edward looked over at the front door and saw Colin striding out to meet him. "You found us okay?"

"Your directions were perfect."

"It's good to see you." Colin embraced him. "You look very well. A little older, but it suits you."

"It's good to see you too. It's been too long."

"We did invite you, you know. For the five-year anniversary, and the ten-year…"

"I know, I'm sorry," Edward shook his head. "I wanted to join you, but work always got in the way." In truth he could have attended both of the previous reunions, but had chosen instead to wait. The time hadn't been right. He'd still been making his way in the world. He'd still been unproven.

"Everyone's dying to see you. Particularly after your deal with Merck—we've been following it in the press. Do you have any bags?" Edward opened the boot and let Colin lift out his Mulberry hold-all and his suit carrier. "James is here already, and George and Casper and their wives. I don't suppose you know the wives, do you?"

"No, I missed the weddings as well as the reunions."

"They're great girls, all of them. And you'll meet Harriet of course."

"Yes, congratulations."

"We can't stay bachelors forever, eh?" Colin smiled at him but Edward ignored the dig.

"Have you set a date?"

"May, next year. Now that you're back in the fold, so to speak, you've no excuse not to be there."

"I wouldn't dream of it. Anyway, I'll be out of a job in a few months, a free man."

"A free man, and rich," Colin smiled.

"That's the plan."

"Come on, I expect you could use a drink. The others will be back soon, they went for a walk. Coz and Flynn are arriving later tonight and the rest will be here tomorrow."

Colin ushered Edward through the front door into a grand hall and dumped his bag and suit carrier on a bench. The house was classically-furnished—full of dark wood and leather sofas, family portraits and old books. In the drawing room, a man was crouched inside a giant fireplace arranging kindling and logs in preparation for the evening.

"Steve, would you mind bringing some Pimms out to the terrace?" Colin asked. "There's a jug already mixed in the fridge." The man stood up and nodded, and Colin led Edward outside onto a broad stone terrace with wrought iron furniture.

"So, fifteen years," Colin said as he slumped into a chair. "Where have you been hiding all that time?"

"Switzerland mostly, Geneva, at least for the last few years. I spent a bit of time in London before that."

"Banking wasn't it?"

"Yes, a boutique Swiss bank, VBG it's called, quite small. They focus mostly on the pharmaceutical industry."

"Didn't you study something along those lines?"

"Cellular pathology, so it was a natural fit... I spent eight years with the bank, raising capital for pharma companies, doing advisory work, M&A, the first two years in London then six in Zurich."

"And then you joined OncoVen?"

"In 2005," Edward nodded. "They took me on as their finance director, I did that for a year and a half, and then they made me CEO."

"Cancer drugs? That's what I read."

"Yeah, for tumours of the stomach and bowels. But it was early-stage when I joined. Dragging a drug through all the clinical trials takes years, and costs a fortune. So that's what I've been doing all this time, steering the firm through all the fund-raising and the trial process."

"And now you've sold it to Merck?"

"We signed the deal two weeks ago."

"That's bloody brilliant."

"Two of our drugs are in phase III clinical development

in the US, which is the last hurdle before they're approved. But we just didn't have the capital to take them further."

"What? You mean to commercialise them?"

"Exactly. To manufacture the drugs at scale and take them to market is a whole new level of investment."

Steve arrived with the Pimms and glasses on a tray. He set it down on the table and poured them both long measures of the drink.

"I read you sold it for US$650m in cash?"

"That's the initial payment."

"There's more?"

"Hopefully... there's another US$750m on top if the drugs perform as we expect."

"If they work you mean?"

"If they reach certain regulatory and sales targets."

"What was your share?" Colin asked.

"Still as blunt as ever," Edward smiled.

"You know it's what everyone wants to know."

"I had four percent of the equity. I put a lot of my own cash into the firm, money I saved from working at the bank."

"What is that? Twenty-six million dollars today... and another thirty mill to come?"

"If the drugs perform as expected."

"Bloody good for you," Colin lifted his glass and clinked it against Edward's.

"And what about you? You're a barrister now?"

"Yes, intellectual property law."

"Highly successful with it too, I hear."

"True Pharaohs," Colin laughed, clinking Edward's glass again, "the pair of us."

"It's still going is it? Back at Cambridge?"

"The Pharaohs? Of course. One joined my chambers last year."

Edward relaxed into his chair and thought back to his days at university. The Pharaohs was a dining club started in the 1920s. Exclusive and private, membership was by invitation only and limited to twenty undergraduate students.

Every September, ten new members were chosen from the second year. They stayed members for two years before graduating at the end of their third year. Numerous judges, politicians, civil servants and scientists had been members. Lord Alan Saunders, the mathematician, had been a Pharaoh, as had Edmund Wellows, the author, and Connor Cartwright, the film director.

"This place is truly magnificent," Edward said, looking out at the views.

"My great grandfather built it in 1912."

"You must come here all the time."

"Sadly, not. It's too much of a trek from London. I spent a lot of time here as a child."

"How lovely to grow up here."

"The weather can be bloody awful at times."

"You know my background was much more humble. My father was an optician in Ashford in Kent. We lived in a semi-detached house. Holidays were a couple of weeks staying with my aunt in Wales," Edward paused.

"Still plagued by class anxieties?"

"No, not at all," Edward laughed. "But looking back, I sometimes wonder why I was invited to join The Pharaohs."

"Potential," Colin said flatly. "Look at what you've become. Somebody saw it in you."

"Has everyone done well? All ten?"

"By and large. George is a banker with JP Morgan. James runs a publishing company, Camden Court Books—they just published Lord Chapman's autobiography. Coz is doing well. He's based in Russia these days, working on some sort of oil venture in Siberia. He flew in especially to be here. Anyway, you can ask them all yourself."

"What about Tennyson?"

"Don't you mean Amber?" Colin laughed.

"That's all long in the past," Edward said. It was true, although his memories had barely faded.

It was more than fifteen years earlier that Edward had first seen Amber. One evening in January during his final year, he had attended a debate at the Cambridge Union Society. The Debating Chamber had been filled with 850 students packed onto leather benches and crammed into the wooden balcony that encircled the room.

The proposition before the chamber that night was "This house believes the world is moving too fast". Speeches were given for and against the motion, before the president opened the debate to the floor. It was then that Edward had noticed Amber. He was sitting on the balcony and Amber was down below. Edward was surprised that she hadn't caught his eye before. Her hair was long, wavy and fiery red, and her figure was slim but attractive. She raised her hand and the president invited her to speak.

"My concern isn't for the present, it's for the future," she had said. "Without question, the world is speeding up. And when the pace of change is constantly accelerating it means that people have less and less certainty about the future. Our horizons get shorter. The result is a culture of ever increasing short-termism. You can see it in the way that companies and markets operate. You can see it in the attitudes of politicians and policymakers. Humanity is becoming obsessed with the short-term. We are abandoning any attempt to take the long view. And yet we need that long view, we need a strategic vision of where humanity is heading. For that reason I support the proposition."

The audience had applauded her point, and Edward had been impressed by her performance. Such confidence, such poise and eloquence, such a striking physical presence.

"They're both fine, as far as I know," Colin continued. "Tennyson's still trading commodities. Amber was a lawyer before she married Tennyson. She's a mother these days—they have two children."

"She's not practicing law any more?"

"No," Colin shook his head. "You should have been at their wedding."

"It was bad timing," Edward lied. "I couldn't get away from work."

"They'll be here tomorrow. Tennyson said they'd arrive in time for lunch."

It was 2.00am by the time Edward climbed into bed. The evening had progressed well, with drinks and dinner and cigars by the fire in the drawing room. Edward was surprised at how little everyone had changed. They looked older, of course, and had matured, but the broad contours of their characters remained. As he dozed into a brandy-induced sleep, Edward was filled with impressions of a slowly eroding landscape. Back at Cambridge, the mountains had been jagged, the soil thin and the rivers fast-rushing over stony beds. Today, the peaks had been smoothed, the earth had grown richer, and the rivers ran deeper and more slowly. But despite these changes, the paths by which Edward had come to know these landscapes had stayed much the same.

The following morning, Edward woke late and lay thinking about the day ahead. Amber and Tennyson would be joining the party, and he felt a knot of excitement. It wasn't that he harboured any hopes of winning her back. It was more that he wanted to show her what he had become since leaving Cambridge. He wanted Amber to know what could have been.

Downstairs, the house was stirring, and Edward joined his friends in the kitchen for coffee and breakfast. Newspapers were piled on the table and many of the party were more in the mood for reading than talking, but Colin was determined they didn't waste the day. Outside, the weather was clear and crisp and he declared that the morning would be spent shooting clay pigeons.

By 11.30am, all of them were up in a field behind the house with shotguns and shooting sticks. Colin had arranged for a table to be set with coffee, and whisky for those who wanted it. Steve—the estate manager—was manning the trap, sending clays arcing out over the valley. Many of the party were experienced shots, and Edward felt something of a fraud taking part, but he held his own. Colin organised them into two teams, and Edward's team lost by only a narrow margin.

As they were packing up and readying to return to the

house, the jarring sound of a car horn rang out repeatedly across the hillside. Down below, a red sports car was racing up the lane to the house.

"Tennyson," Colin said. "Let's head down."

When they reached the house, Tennyson and Amber were already sitting out on the terrace. They rose to greet Colin and the others as they approached.

"Bloody hell!" Tennyson boomed when he saw Edward. "Eddy Tenure, look at you. The prodigal Pharaoh returns!" He threw open his arms and wrapped them around Edward in a bear-hug, lifting him off the ground and swinging him round. Tennyson had been a rugby blue at Cambridge and in the years since then had added girth to his height and breadth. "How the hell are you, old man?"

"I'm well," Edward replied, disengaging from the hug.

"You look good, too good. What's your secret? Skiing I'll bet, all that Swiss mountain air."

"You look well yourself." Edward glanced over Tennyson's shoulder and saw Amber saying hello to some of the others. She was dressed casually in loose cargo pants and a baggy jumper, but Edward could see that her figure looked as impressive as he remembered. And her hair, pinned back with two clips, was still fiery red.

"I can't believe we've found you again, after fifteen years."

"Silly isn't it," Edward turned back to Tennyson.

"I bet you didn't realize how much you'd missed us all until you saw us again?"

"You're right."

"It's always the way isn't it?" Tennyson shrugged. "You get so busy with things and pursuing your career and then you wake up and your life's passed you by. You forget what's important."

"Very true," Edward nodded.

"What's very true?" Amber had joined them. She put one arm around Edward's neck and kissed him on the cheek.

"How easy it is to forget your friends," Tennyson said.

"It is in Edward's case. We missed you at our wedding."

"I'm so sorry," Edward said. "I'd have loved to have been there."

"Give the guy a break," Tennyson said. "That was eight years ago. Water under the bridge."

"I'm only teasing him. It's good to see you Eddy. You look really well."

"As do you. In fact everyone looks well."

"Pharaohs aren't supposed to age are they?" Tennyson laughed. "Our bodies get embalmed and preserved and we live forever."

"Or pickled in your case," Amber smiled at her husband, and turned to Edward. "I must say hello to Harriet, but I'm really looking forward to catching up properly."

A lunch of cold meats and salads and cheese was served outside on the terrace, with a generous supply of wine. The party sat around two tables that ended up with one being mostly men and the other mostly women. Edward wanted to talk to Amber, but she was with the women's table and locked in a lively conversation. Instead, he found himself telling Tennyson about the course of his career and the recent sale of OncoVen to Merck. As for Tennyson, he was full of stories, just as he had always been. Edward learned that, after leaving Cambridge he'd joined his father's commodities trading business in the City, and when his father had died three years earlier, he'd taken over as chief executive.

Edward contributed to the conversation around his table as much as was required, but his mind was elsewhere. From where he was sitting, he could observe Amber without her seeing him. She spoke with passion and animation, just as Edward remembered. And when she listened her expression was focused and full of intensity. Occasionally she laughed, and her seriousness dissolved, but never completely. At Cambridge, Amber had had a playful side, but Edward had always liked her seriousness best.

As he watched, he wondered if some of that ardour had been lost over the past fifteen years. He sensed a certain detachment about her, a preoccupation with other thoughts. Certainly her greeting to him had been much more cursory and less enthusiastic than he was expecting.

The lunch went on long into the afternoon. During the course of the meal, the final two pharaohs arrived with their wives, taking the party to eighteen in total. Only Edward himself and Coz—whose girlfriend had stayed in Russia—were without partners. By 4.00pm, some of the party began to drift away, and Edward heard Amber tell Tennyson that she was going to lie down before the evening began.

The dinner that night, with everybody in black tie, was the showpiece of the weekend, just as it had been at meetings of the Pharaohs during Cambridge days. Back then, the occasions had been men only, with ten students from the second year and ten from the third year. Today, it would be just the ten pharaohs from Edward's intake, plus the eight accompanying partners. Colin announced that everybody should meet back on the terrace at 7.00pm for cocktails, and as the party thinned, Edward also retired to his room.

Just after 6.00pm, Edward was woken by a knock on his door. It was Colin handing out the Pharaoh's bow-ties. These ones were new, but the style was the same as always—silk stripes of gold and burgundy. Edward got up, showered and put on his new dress shirt, dinner jacket, bow-tie and shoes. He looked at himself in the mirror and for a moment saw himself fifteen years earlier, dressed in just the same way. Back then, his future had been so uncertain. He wondered what 22-year-old Edward would have thought of the 37-year-old version. Perhaps pride, he thought, that he had overcome some of his insecurities.

Out on the terrace, Colin had hired a team of caterers who moved around the group serving champagne and canapés. All the Pharaohs were dressed in their bow-ties and dinner jackets, and the women had put on evening gowns. Amber looked striking. She wore a simple halter-net black dress that reached to the ground. Against the black material, her red hair, now worn long and loose, shimmered like coals in the evening sun.

Over dinner, Edward was at last able to talk to her properly. Colin had put the two of them next to each other. The dining room was baronial in its proportions, with a long table capable of seating twenty-two diners. A large fire roared in an ornate stone hearth, and candles burned up and down the table.

Edward asked after Amber's career as a lawyer, and her two children—two girls—who were being looked after by Amber's parents for the weekend. She in turn asked about his life in Geneva and expressed her admiration for the path that his career had taken. The conversation was pleasant enough, but it felt empty to Edward. It was as if they were merely acquaintances. Perhaps that was all that remained after fifteen years with no contact.

By the time the main course was served, a traditional roast lamb, the table had grown boisterous. At regular intervals, a Pharaoh stood and proposed a toast. Some of them noted the success of those at the table, some of them recalled times past at Cambridge, while others celebrated cherished character flaws—Flynn's ability to start a fight (which, being only small, he relied on his friends to fight for him), Tennyson's gambling habit, Caspar's experimental cooking, and George's fascination with "apple wine" (he had recently bought a cider orchard in Somerset). Some of the women around the table made their own toasts, teasing their husbands. And with each toast, Edward noticed that Amber relaxed, and their conversation grew more natural.

"You remember when we met?" Amber asked as the dessert was being served.

"Of course," Edward replied. "In the Members' Bar in the Union. After the debate."

"You were so awkward."

"Awkward, but determined to meet you."

"And very sweet."

In the weeks after the debate, Edward had spent more and more time with Amber, having lunch together, studying in the library, going to the cinema. It wasn't until a month later, after a piano recital staged beneath the soaring arches of the chapel at King's College, that Edward had first kissed her. The music had been by Rachmaninov, and the stirring, troubling notes ringing around in the chapel, followed by the quiet of the frosted night outside, had given Edward the confidence to make his move. It was a moment that had lived with him ever since.

At the time, Edward had wanted more than anything for his liaison with Amber to blossom into a full relationship. But he also knew that he wasn't her only suitor. She also spent time with another student—Phil Tennyson, one of the ten Pharaohs in Edward's year. She had met Tennyson several weeks before Edward, at a lecture, and had started spending more and more time with him too. Both Edward and Tennyson knew about the other—Amber was quite open about the situation—but they moved in different circles, rarely seeing each other except during Pharaohs' dinners.

"You remember towards the end of the Lent term?" Amber asked. "We'd been hanging out for a few months, then one day you completely cut me off. One minute we were close, really good friends. The next I hardly ever saw you."

"I do remember," Edward nodded.

"I never understood at the time why you cut me off."

"I was studying hard and focusing on my exams. Working too hard," Edward paused. "It's a bad habit of mine, working too hard, ignoring my personal life. Even today, getting OncoVen to where it is."

"I don't doubt it," Amber said.

"I'm going to fix it, though, now that I've sold the company," Edward nodded to himself. "I'm planning to take some time out and reassess my life. Decide what's important."

"Good for you," Amber said, watching Edward closely. "But back at Cambridge there was another reason wasn't there? Another reason you shut me out?"

"What do you mean?"

"The Pharaoh's Wager?" Amber let her words hang for a

moment. "With Tennyson?"

"You know about that?"

"I didn't for a long time. But then it came out before my wedding."

"Who told you?"

"Tennyson. He was drunk one night. I was doing the invitation lists and I said I couldn't understand why you'd dropped off the scene so completely."

"I see."

"That's when he told me."

"I'm sorry," Edward shrugged, "I really am. Looking back it feels silly. I lost the bet and I felt I had to honour it."

"You certainly did that."

"I suppose I also lacked confidence. I always thought that you'd opt for Tennyson anyway." Edward felt relieved that Amber knew. At least she understood.

"Maybe you should have had more confidence in yourself," Amber said. "If Tennyson was so sure of himself, he wouldn't have made the bet in the first place."

The Pharaoh's Wager was an institution. At least one, and sometimes two or three, had been staged during each of the twice-yearly weekends that the group had arranged. During Edward's time at Cambridge, the wagers had taken place around shooting, golf, tractor-racing, table-tennis and numerous other sports and pseudo sports.

Each wager resembled a pyramid. It was arranged in five rounds, with ten Pharaohs in the first round, eight in the second, six in the third, until two Pharaohs remained in the final round, with one winner emerging triumphant at the top of the pyramid. Each round carried a stake—be it money or something else entirely—with all the Pharaohs contributing their stake into a pot. Those who were eliminated lost their stakes while the winning Pharaoh kept everything.

For Edward, who lacked the wealth of others in the group, his strategy had often been to lose intentionally in the first round. That way he only lost one stake. The worst outcome was to make it all the way to the final—and in so doing, to have contributed five stakes—but then lose and come away with nothing.

Fifteen years ago, Edward had competed in a Pharaoh's Wager and had experienced the worst of all outcomes. It was a weekend in a country hotel in Worcestershire in late March. It had snowed during the week, and the Cotswold Hills were blanketed in white. The Pharaohs had hired all the rooms in a small 17th century staging inn. Late on the Saturday night, after the black-tie dinner and with all of them flush with wine, the call had gone out for a Pharaoh's Wager. The sport was darts and the game was 301.

Edward remembered every round with absolute clarity. For the first round, the stake was £30, for the second it was £60, for the third it was £120, and for the fourth it was £240. Unusually for Edward, he decided early in the game to compete all the way to the final. Darts was a game he'd played with his father many times in their local pub in Ashford. He felt confident he could hold his own and, sure enough, he made it to the fifth and final round without any trouble.

By that stage, Edward had personally put £450 into the pot—far more than he could afford to lose. But his eye was on winning, and the total value of all the stakes up to that point stood at £2,460. Edward's opponent in the final was Tennyson who was drunker than most, and Edward felt sure he could beat him.

For the final round of the Pharaoh's Wager, Tennyson had proposed not money, but a deal. The stake was Amber. Whoever won would be left free to pursue Amber alone. The loser would stop seeing her, stop calling her, and move on to pastures new. To Edward, himself a little drunk, the deal sounded perfect. His rival for Amber's affections would be removed from the picture, leaving the field clear for him.

"That final round of the wager, I was so confident I'd win," Edward said. "Tennyson was swaying all over the place. I thought it was in the bag."

"What happened?"

"I don't know really. It was close. Tennyson played better

than I was expecting. I had a chance to win it. I was ahead towards the end, but then Tennyson came through. Just luck I think."

"You weren't tempted to break your promise?"

"Sorely tempted, but I gave my word."

"Very honourable of you."

"Yes, but like I said, I never felt sure where I stood with you."

"I always told you what I felt."

"I know, but I thought if you'd truly wanted to be with me, you wouldn't have been seeing Tennyson too."

"We were twenty-one. Going to university was about experimenting, trying out things, not closing off avenues. I thought it was fine so long as there was no deceit, no doing things behind anyone's back."

"You're right, and I'm sorry now. Mostly for myself, but also for you."

"C'est la vie," Amber shrugged. "What's done is done."

Edward noticed her reach for the ring finger on her left hand, an instinctive habit, perhaps nervousness. Only, the finger was bare, and she twisted an imaginary ring.

"You're not wearing a wedding ring," Edward said, nodding towards her hand.

"No," Amber said, and smiled. "It's being repaired."

At the far end of the table, Flynn had stood up on his chair and was clinking his wine glass with a knife and calling for quiet. "Not a toast," he said, pausing for effect, "But a call… for a Pharaoh's Wager."

The table erupted into cheering and shouts and suggestions of what the sport should be. Edward glanced at Amber, but she was staring across the table at her husband, watching as he voiced his own support for the wager. Colin rose and quietened the room.

"As the host, I get to choose," he said. "I nominate English billiards. There's a table next door. Bring your drinks."

"Just what we need," Amber said, looking away from her husband.

Around the table the guests rose to their feet, laughing and talking and grabbing wine bottles and glasses. Edward watched them file out of the dining room.

"Come on, let's get it over with," Amber said finally, when most of the table had left.

In the billiards room, Colin was shouting the rules over the noise of conversation. The first round would see ten Pharaohs compete in five games. Each game would stop when one player reached 50 points. It was a low target, Colin explained, but none of them were expert at billiards, and all of them were drunk. After all five games, the two players with the lowest scores would be eliminated. The remaining eight players would compete in the second round in a similar fashion, with the two lowest scorers dropping out before round three, and so on.

Colin wrote the names of all the Pharaohs onto pieces of paper, folded them and put them into a leather bushman hat. Harriet drew them out and Colin wrote the names on a blackboard on the wall. Edward was up first against George. As the first pair, it was up to them to suggest the wager. Edward let George decide, and he proposed £1,000. All the Pharaohs agreed. The hat was passed round for each of them to deposit the wager into it. Edward, who had suspected that a Wager would feature during the weekend, had £8,000 in cash in his room upstairs. He fetched the money and placed the required amount in the hat.

With the first bets organised, the game got under way. Edward and George took off their jackets. The room was large, with a full snooker table at the centre, lit by an elaborate brass fixture suspended from the roof. Chairs were arranged around the walls, and at one end of the room stood a wooden bar next to the scoreboard. The party watched and cheered and drank as the two men played, with a third Pharaoh calling out the score after each shot.

Edward lost his first game, but scored 37 points. With two other Pharaohs recording worse scores, he was still able to graduate into round two. The stake for the second round was raised to £2,000 and all eight remaining Pharaohs contributed their cash. This time, Edward was pitched against Colin, and once again he lost, with a score of just 34. But again, two other Pharaohs chalked up lower scores, so keeping Edward in the competition.

For the third round, one of the wives suggested a forfeit instead of a cash bet—the two losing Pharaohs would have to strip naked and run round the outside of the house. The bet was warmly welcomed, and this time Edward won his match, beating James 50 to 38. The two losing Pharaohs—James and Colin—duly stripped and raced round the house to the cheers and whooping of the group who accompanied them to the front door.

The fourth round involved just two games, the first was Edward against Flynn, the other Tennyson against George. Flynn suggested the wager should be the watches that each of them were wearing. Much discussion followed over the relative value of each of their timepieces, but the bet was agreed and each of them unbuckled their watch and placed it in the hat. Edward's game was close but he won, beating Flynn 50 to 44. Tennyson's was even closer, but he too prevailed.

The final, then, was a single game between Edward and Tennyson. The first to reach 50 points would be the winner. In the hat lay £26,000 and four expensive watches, with one final stake to be added.

"Just like old times, eh?" Tennyson said, leaning on Edward's shoulder. The ash from his cigar dropped onto Edward's shirt, and Tennyson rubbed it away, leaving a dirty smear of grey across the white. "You remember our darts match? Bloody close wasn't it?"

"Not close enough."

"So you're ready for another shot?"

"Yes," Edward nodded. "What'll it be this time?"

"I get to choose? More wine first I think." Tennyson walked over to the bar and filled his glass, knocked back half of it, and then shouted for the room to be quiet.

"For the final bet," he said, rummaging in his pocket, "I

wager my car, my Porsche 911, against Eddy's car." He held out his keyring and tossed it onto the billiards table.

"Are you sure?" Edward asked, shocked at the size of the bet. "What's that worth? £80,000?"

"It's about the same price as the Jaguar XKR you've got parked outside."

"How old is it?" one of the Pharaohs asked.

"It's in good condition," Tennyson said, his eyes fixed on Edward. "I've had it a year and a half."

The room fell silent and all eyes turned to Edward. He walked forward and picked up Tennyson's car keys from the table, weighing them in his hand. His fingers clasped around the fob and he stroked it as he considered the bet.

"You've had your car a year and a half? It was new when you got it?"

"Yes," Tennyson nodded. "Top of the range, a fantastic motor."

Edward looked down at the keys in his hand, and then around the room, as if seeking guidance from the faces watching him. He looked at Amber, but she was staring at the floor. Calculations and consequences buzzed through his brain. He looked at Tennyson and held out his hand. "I accept."

"Hold on… wait a moment," Colin held up his hands. "That's a lot of money…"

"Too late," Tennyson cut him off. "We've shaken on it."

The atmosphere in the room grew serious. Many of the group stood up and drew closer to the table. The Pharaohs had played for all kinds of stakes in the past, but none as expensive as this. Edward felt sure the tension was even higher given the history that he and Tennyson shared. Nobody mentioned the previous wager of fifteen years earlier, but he sensed that everyone was thinking about it.

The game started well for Edward. In one early break, he scored 22 points. Tennyson played better than expected too, and kept in close touch with Edward's score. The atmosphere made Edward nervous. His hands felt clammy as he gripped the billiard cue, but his play stayed strong. When the scores reached 43 to 39 in Edward's favour, Tennyson let out a roar of frustration.

"Bloody hell it's hot in here," he exclaimed, and the room laughed like steam escaping a pressure valve. "We need another drink. Do you mind Eddy? A quick pause?"

"No," Edward shook his head. It was his turn next and the lie of the balls on the table looked promising. He waited as Colin filled Tennyson's glass, and those of the others clustered around the bar. Tennyson drank almost the whole glass in one go and returned to the table.

Edward leant over the table and lined up his first shot—a cannon, taking his score to 45. The next shot was an easy pot on Tennyson's cue ball, earning him another two points. He needed just three more for victory. The red ball was well-positioned over the centre pocket and Edward had a simple shot to sink it and earn himself the winning points.

He leant over the table and lined up his cue. The shot was straightforward, the sort you'd never bet against anybody missing. Edward gripped his cue and drew it back, but his hands felt sticky and he stood up.

"It is hot isn't it?" he said, drying his hands on his shirt. The room was silent, all the faces watching in stunned fascination. Tennyson's face, only moments earlier aglow with wine, had turned white and pale. Near the bar, Amber's expression seemed distant and blank, as if she had already given up on her husband's chances and had resolved to put a brave face on the defeat.

Edward studied all of them closely, he glanced back at Amber, trying to read her expression, and then looked at the table. He leant down, lined up his shot and struck. The room erupted into gasps. His cue ball narrowly missed the red, hit the cushion, and bounced back into space.

"You missed!" Tennyson said, "You bloody missed. Two penalty points for me."

"That takes the score to 47 to Edward, 41 to Tennyson," Colin said.

Tennyson leant over the table and potted the red that

Edward had missed, lifting his score to 44. Two cannons followed in quick succession, taking him to 48. And now it was Tennyson's turn to line up for the winning shot. He took his time, setting up to pot Edward's cue ball. His strike was strong, and the ball ricocheted off the pocket cushions twice, but then dropped in. Tennyson straightened and looked over at Edward.

"I'm sorry mate," he said, "but that's it."

"Congratulations," Edward said, shaking his hand and patting him on the back. "A worthy winner. You played well."

"You almost had me with that red. I must admit, my heart was going like a stagecoach. Bloody hell!"

"Eddy, really bad luck," Colin said, putting his arm around his shoulder. "I really thought you'd take the game back then."

"The pressure," Edward laughed.

"I know, we could all feel it. Come on, have a drink."

"I will. Let me get some air first. I need to cool down." Edward slipped out of the room and made his way out onto the terrace. The night air was cold and cloudless and above the black hills the stars were glittering in their thousands. Edward watched them and let his mind empty and relax. He felt good, strangely good for a man who had just lost his car.

Back inside the house, the mood in the billiards room had returned to its former gaiety. Edward stopped in the corridor outside and listened to the talk. Tennyson was holding court and calling for champagne. In a different part of the house, somebody had found a piano and was playing Jerusalem while several others sang the words to the hymn.

Edward smiled at the sounds and crept upstairs to his room. He took off his socks and shoes and shirt and opened the window. He shivered in the cool air, but it felt good, refreshing, cleansing. He lay on the bed in the darkness, thinking about the evening, until his thoughts were disturbed by a knock on the door. He sat up and watched as it opened and Amber walked in.

"Edward, are you here?"

"Yes," he said, switching on the bedside lamp. Amber closed the door and sat on the bed beside Edward.

"You missed that shot on purpose didn't you?" she asked. "You could have won the game and you chose to lose."

"Yes."

"Why?"

"Tennyson's in financial difficulties isn't he?"

"Why do you say that?"

"A few things, I suppose. The way you were acting and some of the things you said."

"Like what?"

"Your wedding ring…"

"I told you, it's being repaired."

"But you're not wearing any jewellery at all, nothing. It can't all be at the repairers. And your children staying with your parents—no au pair, no nanny. That's not Tennyson's style."

"It's a bit tenuous isn't it?"

"The thing that confirmed it for me was the car. When I picked up his keys I noticed the fob, the key ring. It was from Robert Dickenson Performance Motors. I've used them myself. His Porsche is a hire-car, isn't it?"

"So?"

"He said he'd owned it for a year and a half, but he can't have done if it's a rental. He hired the Porsche to keep up appearances, didn't he?"

Amber looked down at her feet for a long time, then up at Edward. "You're right, of course. The business is doing badly. He made some big bets and the markets moved the wrong way. We've been struggling for a while now, and it's getting worse."

"Tonight's winnings should help a bit."

"The problem's bigger than that," Amber shook her head. "Anyway, why did you accept the bet if you knew Tennyson was bluffing?"

"I wanted to teach him a lesson. I wanted payback for fifteen years ago."

"But you didn't go through with it?"

"No," Edward shook his head. "I came close, believe me. I wanted to sink that red. But as I looked around the room, I imagined the pain it would cause—to you, and your children, and the humiliation for Tennyson. I couldn't do it."

"If the tables were turned, Tennyson would have sunk that red. He can't bare losing."

"I know," Edward nodded.

"Do you ever wonder what would have happened if you'd won that wager fifteen years ago?"

"Always," Edward said. "It still haunts me."

Amber lifted her hand and ran her fingers through Edward's hair, stroking his cheek. She leaned over and kissed him, letting her lips linger on his, before standing and locking the door. She returned to the bed. Edward stood and drew Amber towards him.

"I can't believe you lost you car," Amber said as she kissed Edward.

"I don't care," Edward whispered. He only owned one car, his old Renault in Geneva, and it was worth next to nothing. Tennyson was welcome to have it. As for knowing what to replace it with, Edward would need to rent a few more models before he made a decision. The Jaguar XKR he'd hired for the weekend—the car that Tennyson had assumed he was playing for—wasn't due back with Robert Dickenson for another two days but Edward had already decided it was a little showy for his taste.

Downstairs, the party had shifted from the billiards room to the drawing room where a crowd was clustered around the piano. George was sitting on the stool, banging out show tunes as the group found its voice and filled the house with song. Tennyson was among them, swaying with the music, and organising drinks from one of the hired serving staff. He felt good. Nothing was better than staring down disaster, staring into the abyss, and coming away a winner.

"Here," he said, as a waiter returned with a new bottle of wine. Tennyson plucked a gold watch from the hat on top of the piano and dropped it into the waiter's shirt pocket. "Great job this evening."

9

SEPTEMBER: TO EVERYTHING THERE IS A SEASON

Half way along a row of semi-detached houses on the edge of Sedbergh, Jim Fleeting parked his car and rushed into his back garden. His wife took the keys and opened the front door of the house, while Jim slipped down the side and into the long thin garden that separated his house from the fields and hills beyond.

The first third of the garden was a narrow lawn surrounded by flowerbeds, while the final third was a vegetable plot. In between was Jim's bonsai collection. Two rows of diminutive trees growing out of porcelain pots stood on waist-high wooden benches. A flag-stone path ran between them.

Jim had spent the past three weeks in Scotland visiting his wife's family and relatives near Fort William. It had rained extensively during their break, but that didn't mean it had rained in Sedbergh, and the shallow pots in which the bonsai grew could quickly dry out. It took decades to grow a true bonsai, but just one week without rain could kill the trees. Jim had asked his neighbour to keep an eye on them, but he still felt anxious.

Jim worked his way down the line, inspecting each of his thirty-two trees, examining the leaves for dehydration and insect damage. One or two of them needed pruning, and Jim made a note to remove the training wires on the branches of some of his trees so that they didn't cut into the thickening wood. Jim's most prized tree, a trident maple, was 116 years old and had come from Japan. He had owned it for just eleven of those years—it had been a gift on his twenty-first birthday—but he hoped it would live for at least another century, long after he was dead. Trees were a majesterial presence on the earth, their lives far longer and nobler than those of humans, and bonsai were no exception.

"All the antiques still alive?" his wife asked when he returned to the house.

"Yes," Jim nodded. "They look well watered."

"I told you not to worry."

"They need some pruning and a bit of TLC, but nothing serious."

"What about your other favourite antique?"

"Rev Mason?"

"Who else?" his wife smiled at him, shaking her head. "Are you going to see him later?"

"I said I'd take him to church tomorrow. He won't have been for three weeks."

"What about lunch afterwards? Do you want to bring him round here?"

"Yes, he'd like that." Jim put on the kettle and set out two mugs. "I think I'll unpack our stuff and then drive into Kendal to pick up his watch. They said it would be ready by now."

"He'll be grateful, I'm sure."

Later that afternoon, as Jim drove the ten miles into Kendal, he passed the school in Sedbergh where he and his wife worked—he as a cook and she as assistant librarian. The Michaelmas term was starting on Wednesday, in four days' time, but both he and his wife would be back on Monday with all the other staff, getting the place ready before the students returned.

On the outskirts of Kendal, Jim passed the retirement home where Rev Mason lived, but he didn't stop. He'd be there in good time the following morning to pick him up for the 10.30 service at St Andrew's church. He was looking forward to catching up with him and telling him about the trip to Scotland.

In the jewellers, Jim inspected the watch, making sure that it had been repaired properly. Rev Mason would be delighted to get it back. The old man was eighty-three, and as he'd aged he had become fixated on knowing the time. He checked his watch constantly, as if he had eggs on the boil and was determined they shouldn't overcook. It wasn't that he had appointments to miss—Jim and his wife were his only regular visitors. And the routines in the retirement home, marked out by meals and programmes on Radio 4, never altered. Jim wondered if it was monotony that caused him to watch the time with such intensity, in the way that zoo animals pace their cages. Occasionally it felt as if he were counting down the hours and minutes to a final fixed point that only he knew.

Two weeks before Jim's holiday, Rev Mason's watch had stopped, causing him great consternation. Jim had offered to get it repaired—a process that required the jeweller to send it to London and took five weeks. While it was away, Jim had lent the reverend his own watch, a gold Breitling that had come into his possession. Occasionally Jim worked part-time for a local catering company, and one weekend he'd been helping out at a dinner party when one of the guests had given him the watch as a tip. It was an attractive timepiece and Jim was looking forward to getting it back from the reverend.

Back at home, Jim opened the shed at the bottom of his garden and took out his box of bonsai tools. If Rev Mason was coming to lunch, he'd be sure to inspect the trees and Jim wanted them looking at their best. He walked down the row of trees, watering the soil and roots lightly in preparation for applying fertilizer. He sprayed the leaves too, to displace insects and spiders.

Most of the trees were trained in the informal upright

style that Jim favoured. The form seemed typically English to him, mimicking the trees that grew in the valleys all around. But he also had more adventurous creations that he thought of as representing the stunted, gnarled shapes of mountain trees, the sort that survived in thin soil on a windswept cliff face.

Three of the maples in his collection were grown with exposed roots twisted round protruding rocks. Jim also had several bonsai pots that contained a handful of trees each, grown to resemble an isolated copse on a remote hilltop—one of larch trees, and the other of hornbeam. Perhaps the most striking tree was an evergreen Chinese juniper grown in the cascade style, with its knotted trunk arched over the side of the pot and the pads of foliage growing below.

Almost all of Jim's trees grew out of hand-painted porcelain pots that had once belonged to Rev Mason. It was he who had introduced Jim to the art of bonsai growing when he was fifteen years old. And it was he who had given Jim the 116-year-old Japanese maple for his twenty-first birthday. The pots had come several years later.

Before he'd retired, Rev Mason had been the local vicar for the parish of Sedbergh, Cautley and Garsdale. As a schoolboy, Jim had been a member of his choir in St Andrew's Church. He still remembered the fascination he'd felt at seeing the bonsai trees that Rev Mason sometimes brought into the church. Jim had pestered him to share the secrets of how to grow such wonders, and the reverend and his wife—herself a keen gardener until her death nine years ago—had introduced him to the world of replicating nature in miniature.

The antique Japanese maple that Jim now owned had been one of a large collection of trees that Rev Mason had grown and collected during his life—many of them from Japan itself. Apart from his church work, the reverend's bonsai collection had been his crowning passion. He had taken them to garden shows, displayed them at fetes and festivals, decorated his church with them, and filled his garden to bursting with them.

That is, until four years ago when he had moved into a

retirement home. Samuel, the reverend's son, had persuaded him to make the move. Samuel worked in London as a biology professor at London University and visited his father just twice a year. It was hardly enough to keep an eye on an ailing old man. A retirement home, he had argued, was the only answer. And that meant getting rid of the trees, for they wouldn't fit into the small room in a care home.

Samuel was fifty, unmarried, and took little interest in his father. He had the air of an academic, aloof and cold. When Jim was feeling charitable, he regarded Samuel as absentminded and otherworldly. When he was feeling less forgiving, Jim thought him selfish and heartless.

Jim remembered the trauma that had accompanied the fate of the trees. Rev Mason had wanted to give them away to the local community, but Samuel had objected, arguing that they should sell them. The arguments had gone on for months, and Jim had witnessed one altercation first-hand when visiting the reverend's house. Samuel had arrived from London, bringing with him a news story he had discovered on the internet.

"I did some research and look what I found," Samuel said, pulling a printed copy of the story from his briefcase. "Back in 1999, there was an auction of Bonsai trees at Sotheby's. It was by a German collector, Helmut Ruger. Have you heard of him?"

"No," Rev Mason shook his head.

"He sold 25 bonsai trees in one lot. The most expensive of them was valued at £50,000."

"£50,000?" the reverend repeated. "Was it made of gold?"

"Here, read for yourself."

The old man read the story and then passed it to Jim. The tree was a 600-year-old Japanese yew known as "The Tree of the Emperor's Gaze". The tree had been grown in Otaru in the north of Japan and had caught the eye of Emperor Meiji in the 1880s. The emperor visited the town every year to inspect the herring catch, and on each visit he had insisted that the tree was placed in his hotel room for the duration of his stay.

"I don't have anything that old," Rev Mason had said. "My oldest is about 200 years."

"But you've got many more than 25 trees. You must have at least eighty of them."

"I don't want to sell them."

"Retirement homes are expensive," Samuel had insisted.

"I've got a pension," Rev Mason objected, "and I can sell my house."

"You could live for another twenty years. You need to have money just in case."

"You forgot the words 'I hope'," the Rev replied.

"What?"

"You hope I'll live for another twenty years."

"Yes, yes," Samuel had said. "Hopefully you will. But you'll need as much money as possible so that you're looked after."

"They're like children to me, you know. I've shaped each leaf and branch of every one of them."

"They won't fit in the retirement home."

"But if I give them to the church or to the council, or to Jim here, I could still see them."

"But think of the money they'll bring in, money that you need."

"Is that all that matters to you? The money?"

"Don't be bloody-minded. I'm just thinking of your best interests."

Jim had kept out of the discussion, feeling uncomfortable at being in the room. He had known how heartbroken Rev Mason would be to lose the trees—they had become his lifelong companions, infused not only with his own passion and labour, and that of his wife, but with the efforts of countless other growers who had nurtured the trees before him.

Rev Mason's interest in bonsai growing had been sparked by a trip to Japan in 1966. He'd been 37 years old at the time, working as a sales rep for a collective of Scottish whiskey distillers. During his trip to Tokyo, David Mason—as he was known before joining the church—had noticed a collection of bonsai trees in a park close to his hotel. He'd been instantly drawn to the dignity of the trees and the way they captured the essence not only of a fully-grown tree, but of its landscape too. Though small, the trees were serious and weighty, with as much presence as a tree a hundred times larger.

Jim knew and understood the reverend's deep relationship with the trees. In many ways it was an aesthetic link. But equally, it was a spiritual one too, a connection to the awe of great landscapes and the power of nature. Trees were a path into peace and meditation and contemplation. Jim found it strange that Samuel couldn't see those things in his father.

In the end, Samuel had won through. The trees had been auctioned, fetching £16,000 in total—money that Samuel had kept himself and disbursed on his father's behalf when needed.

Jim had visited the old man many times in the final days before his charges were packed into a van and driven away. Even though he was losing the trees, the reverend had worked to the end keeping them trim and neat and watered. He had even repotted all of them in clean new pots, saying he wanted the trees to look at their best, and giving the old pots to Jim for his own trees. Jim had been delighted to receive them. The pots were stained and one or two were a little chipped, but Jim liked the designs. Some showed serpentine dragons painted in blue and white. Others depicted rustic Japanese landscapes—of rice fields, rivers, mountains and villages—painted in red.

After Rev Mason moved into his retirement home, his son had let him keep just three of his bonsai—all that could be fitted onto the ledge of the sole window in the reverend's bedroom. But rather than providing comfort, Jim felt they acted more as a reminder to the old man of all that he had lost—a whole forest of endeavour and dedication and history and beauty, sold to the highest bidder.

Jim finished watering and fertilizing his trees, and took out his bonsai shears. Pruning was a delicate task and Jim studied the form of each of his trees before snipping at errant branches that had sprouted during the past three weeks. He needed to retain the current shape of each canopy, but always with an eye to the future and a view of how the shape was to evolve in the years ahead. Once the pruning was finished, Jim fetched a bucket of warm water and washing-up liquid and a cloth and scrubbed the bonsai pots of dust and dirt so that the pictures on the sides showed cleanly.

Autumn would be arriving soon, and as Jim knelt down to survey his trees at the correct level, he felt a pang of excitement at the changes to come. The leaves that had sprouted with such luminous and youthful green in the spring, and which had darkened and thickened over the summer, would turn orange and russet and red. While the evergreens would continue unaffected, autumn was arguably the most dramatic time for the deciduous trees. Rev Mason always declared it his favourite time of year, and Jim agreed.

He stood up and packed away his tools and left the garden. He felt good, full of the quiet satisfaction that accompanied a world that was ordered and under control.

The following morning, Jim polished his shoes, put on his suit and tie and readied himself for church. It was 9.00am when he set off in his car, driving out into the overcast day to pick up Rev Mason. He tucked the reverend's watch into his pocket and kissed his wife good-bye, arranging to see her in the church in an hour's time.

Twenty minutes later, Jim parked in front of The Pines Retirement Home for the Elderly. The place made him shudder inwardly each time he visited. Inside, the halls smelled too strongly of air-freshener, and the decoration was functional rather than friendly, with grey carpet tiles on the floors, drab reproduction prints on the walls, and lonely plants filling empty corners.

Jim strode through the reception area and bounded up the stairs to the first floor. Rev Mason's room was at the end of a corridor and Jim knocked loudly on the door, waited for several seconds, then pushed it open.

At first, Jim was confused. The room was empty, stripped clean of all signs of habitation. All the furniture was gone, save for the bed, a night table and an armchair. The white walls were bare, apart from a handful of naked picture hooks. The floor was an empty expanse of carpet.

Jim turned back into the corridor to check he had the right room. The number on the door—09—was the right one, and the position at the end of the corridor was correct. Jim went back into the room and pushed open the bathroom door. Inside, the white bathroom fittings and chrome handrails around the loo and bath gleamed with sterile cleanliness, but all signs of the reverend had been wiped clean. No towel on the rail, no dressing gown on the door, no soap and shampoo on the bath, no medicine on the shelves.

Jim sat on the bed as dark realisation set in. The excitement he had felt at seeing the reverend drained into a hollowness that grew and deepened and filled his mind. He felt raw and angry. He looked at the window ledge where the reverend's three bonsai trees had once stood. He pictured the old man sitting in the armchair, the radio playing in the background, as he sprayed the gentlest of mists onto the foliage of his trees, his concentration as intense as if the placement of each atomized droplet of water was key to the health of the tree.

Could the reverend have moved room? Jim jumped up and made his way downstairs to the reception counter. But as he approached, he knew his old friend was gone. The woman behind the counter was called Becky, a retired nurse who Jim had come to know from his regular visits. When she saw Jim, her expression turned to sadness.

"I'm so sorry," she said as Jim approached.

"When?" Jim asked. "What happened?"

"He had a stroke, two weeks ago."

"Nobody called me…"

"We tried, but there was no answer."

"I was on holiday," Jim said.

"There was nothing you could have done. Nothing anyone could have done."

"But…"

"He was a wonderful man. One of the nicest. We'll miss him here, all of us."

"I suppose you must get used to this sort of thing, working here." Jim felt awkward and didn't know what to say. Rev Mason would have known. He always knew the right word for everyone he met, the bereaved, the newlyweds, the troubled, the sick. Jim had never appreciated how hard it was to respond to the emotional trials of life. He'd never recognised that skill in the reverend, until now.

"Is there a funeral planned?" he asked.

"It took place last week."

"So quickly?"

"His son was here, Samuel. He organised it."

"Which church did they do it in?"

"I don't know," Becky shrugged. "I'm sure someone here will know. I can find out if you like?"

"Yes... How did Samuel even know who to invite? To the funeral I mean?"

"He was very businesslike. He came up from London, cleared out Rev Mason's things, organised the funeral, and left immediately afterwards."

"I wish I'd been here. I feel like I didn't get to say goodbye."

"He left a letter for you, I've got it here somewhere." Becky flipped through the papers in a filing tray, and then turned and opened a cupboard behind the reception counter.

"A letter? From Samuel?"

"No, from Rev Mason."

"He wrote it after his stroke?"

"I don't think so. The doctors said he died very quickly. We found him in his bed, it happened at night. Here it is." She pulled out a brown A4 envelope and passed it to Jim. "He must have written it before the stroke. His son found it in his room and asked us to give it to you."

The lettering on the envelope was in the familiar spidery scrawl of the reverend's handwriting. It said: "For the attention of Jim Fleeting", with his name underlined.

Jim tucked the envelope under his arm and put his hand in his pocket. Inside, his fingers felt the shape of the reverend's watch. He pulled it out and stared at it. He wondered what had happened to his own watch. He presumed Samuel would have it by now. He was welcome to it. He'd rather have the reverend's watch as something to remember him by. He felt sure that Samuel wouldn't mind.

Jim went out to his car and sat in the driver's seat, staring at the envelope. His mind was blank. He didn't know what to do. He sat for half an hour, staring at the envelope. That was it. He would never spend another minute with Rev Mason. They'd never share another autumn together, never glory in another spring. Jim wished he could go back and tell the reverend things that had never been said. How much the man had meant to him. How much of an influence he'd played in his life. The value of his quiet guidance. Jim had never imagined a time without the reverend, and now it felt as if the yardstick to his life had been removed. How would he measure his accomplishments now?

Jim opened the seal of the envelope. Inside was a catalogue from Sotheby's auction house, dated 2004. A folded piece of writing paper was sticking out from halfway through the catalogue. Jim pulled out the paper. It was a letter from the reverend, dated September 2009—three years earlier, and soon after he had moved into the retirement home.

> "Dear Jim," the letter began. "You will know the famous prayer from Ecclesiastes 3:1-8. To everything there is a season, a time for every purpose under the sun. A time to be born and a time to die; a time to plant and a time to pluck up that which is planted… If you are reading this, then my time has come to die. I do so, happy that I have lived my life with purpose and in peace, and my sincerest wishes are that you may achieve the same in your life. Your companionship has meant the world to me. Your patience and support for an old man have been more

valuable than you can know. You have been like a son to me, and my prayers will remain with you forever. Yours, Rev David Mason."

Jim flicked open the catalogue to the page where the letter had been placed. There, in glossy pictures, were five bonsai pots, all of them identical to the ones the reverend had given to Jim four years earlier. Jim scanned through the description. They had been created and hand-painted by a Japanese artist called Tsukinowa Yusen who was born in 1908. The text said he was famous for his work in many media, including wood cuts and paintings, but that his most highly valued work were his hand-painted bonsai pots, with their rich depictions of Japanese villages and landscapes.

The guide price for the five pots in the catalogue, which were being sold as a single lot, was £32,000. Back at home, Jim had at least twenty of them.

10

OCTOBER: HISTORY REPEATS ITSELF

Professor Samuel Mason ambled into the lecture theatre, and placed his laptop and mug of coffee on the desk at the front. Rising away from him were tiered rows of seats where students were finding their places and talking and taking out paper and pens from their bags.

Samuel ignored them as he plugged in his computer and set it up for the lecture. Some of his faculty colleagues found inspiration in the potential of a new university term, with a fresh collection of minds hungry to learn. But for Samuel, he regarded his students more as a necessary evil. His true interest lay in research, in his work decoding the molecular clocks that functioned inside cells, and how they regulated the activity of those cells. Teaching undergraduate students was simply the price that came with a life dedicated to research.

And yet, while the professor found teaching a chore, he couldn't help but strive to do it well. He wanted the students to admire him and his passion. He wanted his subject to be respected and his lectures to be praised. He recognised it as a vanity, an intellectual vanity, but he forgave himself for it. He had little else to show for himself. Being fifty-five years old, balding, and overly slim, he had long since lost interest in his appearance.

"Right, let's get started," Samuel said, quietening the room. He pulled an old gold watch from his pocket and held it up in front of the audience. The watch had belonged to his father before he'd died, although Samuel had never noticed it before his death.

"For the next few lectures, we're going to talk about time, and I wanted to start by thinking about this watch. As you all know, it's a product of the Industrial Revolution. Before the 1700s, men and women told the time by natural phenomena. Our lives were governed by the rotation of the earth and the rising and setting of the sun. It was done that way for millennia."

Samuel stared at the students. The keen attention that came with the start of a new term was clear in their faces. In the front row, one girl showed an especially keen interest. She had long, sandy brown hair, and tanned skin. She looked Mediterranean, and her expression was a curious smile, almost flirtatious. Samuel looked at her for a second and felt sure he recognised her.

"After the Industrial Revolution, however, we came up with all sorts of new ways to keep track of time. Pocket watches, then wrist watches like this one, then digital watches. Today we have hydrogen maser clocks that are so accurate, they lose just one second every thirty-two million years. So we became very clever at measuring time. We no longer needed to see the sun to know what time it was," Samuel put the watch down on the desk. The girl in the front row was still smiling at him.

"But the Industrial Revolution did much more than that. We started producing all sorts of other technologies. Technologies that meant our days no longer needed to be governed by the old 24-hour cycle. Look around you. Electric lights meant that we could work through the night. Trains and planes meant that we could travel at night with no concerns about safety. Sophisticated guidance systems and GPS meant we didn't get lost in the dark. Telephones and the internet meant we could communicate with anyone, anywhere, at any time.

"We developed and popularized psychoactive drugs so that we could stay awake when, in the past, we would have slept. Take this coffee here in front of me, full of caffeine. Or take that can of Red Bull," Samuel pointed to a student in the audience. "Were it not for that Red Bull, you might well be asleep now."

The students laughed. The girl in the front row laughed too, perhaps a little too exaggeratedly, Samuel thought. Where had he seen her before? Why did she seem so familiar?

"In short, we have developed countless technologies that have the power to kill off the old 24-hour cycle of our forefathers. But the thing is, nothing has changed at all. Humans still stick to a 24-hour schedule. It doesn't matter whether you work during the day, or you do shift work at night, or you're an airline pilot travelling across time zones, all our bodies run on a 24-hour cycle.

"At a large scale, we perform certain functions, like sleeping and eating, at roughly the same time every day. And the same is true at a molecular scale too, be it the time when our body temperature is hottest or coldest, the times when we release hormones, the cycles of cell regeneration, or the activity levels in our brains. Every 24 hours, our bodies exhibit the same patterns of activity at the same times. Technology has tried to change us, but it has failed. Our essential internal rhythms and our adherence to a 24-hour cycle have stayed the same.

"Those daily rhythms are, of course, called circadian rhythms. The study of these daily cycles, and the body clocks within us that drive them, is what's known as chronobiology, and that's what we're going to spend the next few weeks focusing on."

Samuel fired up his slide show from the laptop and continued with the lecture. For the next hour, he took the students gradually deeper into the subject, setting out the basics of how biological clocks worked and their importance to the functioning of both animals and plants. The students stayed engaged, and Samuel was pleased with their response.

What troubled him, though, was the girl in the front row. He had seen her before. Indeed, he had seen many of the students in the room before—they were in their second year, and he recognised them from around the campus. But this girl was more significant and he couldn't work out why. The professor puzzled it over while he was talking, occasionally staring at her, but never for more than a second or two, and never acknowledging her smile, or the languid way she combed her hair back with her fingers. It wasn't until the lecture was drawing to a close, that he realised who she was.

"So when you get home tonight, and your body tells you you're feeling tired, don't ignore it," Samuel said, checking his watch and putting it in his jacket pocket. "This capitalist system of ours wants to turn us into perpetual machines that never stop working and consuming and working and consuming. But sleep—eight hours of it—is an essential part of our circadian rhythm. Alright, that's it for today."

Chatter rose up among the students as they packed away their things and started to file out of the auditorium. Several of them thanked the professor as they left, and another stopped to clarify a point from the lecture, but soon the room was almost empty. Samuel turned off his laptop and readied to leave when he noticed the girl from the front row waiting for him by the door.

"I loved your lecture," she said as he approached the door. Her English carried a hint of an accent.

"It's kind of you to say so."

"I'm intrigued by the whole field of chronobiology."

"Really?"

"Yes, very much. I read your profile on the faculty website. Your research sounds fascinating."

"Which areas?" Samuel asked. He felt skeptical about her interest.

"The work you're doing with photoreceptors, and how

they regulate circadian rhythms."

"I see," Samuel nodded. Perhaps he had misread her. "The research is re-opening questions that until recently were considered all but answered. There's so much about photosensory neurones that we really don't understand yet."

"I'm Consuela," the girl held out her hand, "Consuela Alba."

"You're Spanish?" Samuel asked, tucking the laptop under his other arm so that he could shake her hand. He needn't have asked, for he knew the answer already.

"Half-English and half-Spanish. I grew up in Madrid."

"It's very nice to meet you. I'm sure we'll have lots of opportunity to discuss all of this much more in the coming weeks."

"I hope so," Consuela said. "I think we're going to have a lot of fun on this course." She flashed her smile at him, stuck out her chest, and for a moment Samuel thought she was going to lean up and kiss him. "Until next week," she said, spinning on her heel and skipping out of the room.

Samuel didn't see Consuela again until the next lecture a week later, but she stayed in his thoughts. He had heard many stories about her, but it was only on meeting her that the stories crystalised and became real to him. He understood now how certain events had come to pass, and how certain situations had arisen. Consuela had a dangerous ease about her, an openness that put you off guard and drew you in. She was physically alluring, but not overly so. It was that dangerous combination of being attractive enough so that men desired her, yet not so attractive that she seemed unobtainable. Men looked at her, wanted her, and were confident they could have her.

During the following lecture, Consuela sat in the same place in the front row. All through the lecture, she watched Samuel with rapt attention, her disarming smile ever present. This time, Samuel allowed himself a quick smile in return to acknowledge their former meeting, but otherwise he tried to ignore her. He had a strong suspicion about her, and in a strange way felt vulnerable. Once again, after the lecture Consuela hung back to talk to him.

"You have a wonderful way of bringing your subject to life," she said.

"Really?" Samuel replied, wary of her approach.

"So many of my lecturers have no spark. I know they love their research, but they can't translate their enthusiasm. They come across as boring and dry."

"Wait till we get deeper into the biochemistry, then you might change your mind," Samuel laughed. Self-deprecation was his natural defense to a compliment.

"I doubt it," Consuela continued in her breezy way. "I'm looking forward to it."

"Good," Samuel felt lost for what to say next. He knew her flattery was a dangerous trap, and was keen to prevent it going any further. He gestured to the door. "Shall we?"

"Yes," Consuela lifted the strap of her bag onto her shoulder and walked with Samuel out into the corridor. "Bye then," she said, "I'm looking forward to next week already."

The third lecture proceeded in much the same way as the first two, with Consuela hanging off his every word. Samuel found himself torn between doubting the sincerity of her compliments, and yet trying to make his lecture as entertaining as possible in order to live up to her false tributes. As the lecture drew to a close an anxiety spread over him, for he knew that she would once again wait for him after the auditorium had cleared.

"Very enjoyable," she said, when the two of them were alone.

"You don't have to say that, you know," Samuel said. "I'm glad you're enjoying the lectures, but there's no need to thank me."

"I know," Consuela nodded, "I'm sorry if I made you uncomfortable. I just get excited by it all."

"It's okay." Samuel picked up his things and started for the door. Consuela walked alongside him.

"Is it true that you're overseeing the second-year research

project?"

"Yes," Samuel nodded. Was this what it was all leading up to?

"I've been thinking a lot about what I wanted to focus my project on. I'm thinking about exploring some of the new ideas emerging in chronobiology."

"You don't have to decide for a few weeks yet."

"I wanted to start developing my ideas early."

"Well that's sensible I suppose."

"I know you're very busy," Consuela put her hand on his arm and stopped before the door. "I wondered if you'd have some time to discuss the ideas I have for my project."

"I don't know…"

"It wouldn't take long. Perhaps half an hour? I'd really appreciate some expert insight."

"Half an hour?"

"No more, I promise. How about Friday?"

"I don't finish until six on Friday…"

"Perfect," Consuela flashed her smile at Samuel. "Shall we say 6.15pm?"

"In my study?"

"Sure," Consuela nodded. "Or we could do it over a drink instead?"

"A drink?"

"Why not? It's the end of the week after all. My treat. You know Bentham's wine bar?"

"Yes…"

"So it's a date? 6.15pm on Friday?"

Samuel hesitated. Her methods were so transparent. How had others fallen for it, he wondered? Surely they hadn't been taken in by her charms? Surely they hadn't believed her? Perhaps it was time to put a few things straight to this girl, to let her see a different side to her deceptions.

"Sure," Samuel nodded. "Bentham's at 6.15pm."

By the time Friday afternoon arrived, Samuel was feeling nervous. He was unaccustomed to meeting women for drinks, and the rendezvous with Consuela came with added pressure.

If she genuinely wanted to discuss her research ideas, then he'd be happy to help her. But if, as he suspected, other motives lay behind their meeting, then he had a few things to say to her. He'd thought carefully about the matter and had prepared his response.

Bentham's was tucked into the basement of a terrace of white stucco-fronted houses. The street above was lined with trees that were shedding their leaves as autumn set in. A chill wind blew down the street, whipping the leaves into eddies and piling them into corners and gutters. But inside the bar it was warm. The lights were low, and the atmosphere was lively, full of office workers toasting the end of the week. Samuel checked all the tables and saw that Consuela hadn't arrived yet. He found a table at the back of the bar and pulled his watch from his pocket. She was late. He'd give her ten minutes, he decided, and then leave. In the end, he waited until 6.40pm.

"I'm so sorry to keep you waiting," she said breathlessly, "I couldn't get a taxi, and the traffic was awful. Typical Friday. I would have called, but of course I don't have your number."

"You didn't come from school?"

"No, I went home to get changed." She took off her coat and threw it over the back of her chair. Underneath, she was dressed in a red cocktail dress, with black stockings and high heels. Her sandy hair was tied up in a ponytail.

"You look very smart, are you going somewhere later?"

"No," Consuela smiled. "No plans yet. Have you ordered a drink? They have a lovely Priorat here."

"That sounds pleasant."

Consuela signaled to a waiter and ordered a bottle.

"There's no point ordering just a glass is there?"

"No," Samuel agreed. He noticed a number of the men in the bar were watching their table, or rather watching Consuela. He felt self-conscious sitting across from her. He wondered what they thought. That she was his girlfriend? His daughter? He looked across at Consuela. "Why are you studying biology?" he asked.

"It interests me."

"That's it?"

"Is there a better reason?"

"No."

"Actually, I'm not being entirely honest. There is another reason. My father runs a crop science business in Spain…"

"Crop science?"

"Seeds, fertilizer, insecticide. It's specialised though, not for mainstream farming. Mostly ornamentals—flowers and orchids, and a few other lines. I want to take over the business one day."

"Is that what your father wants?"

"Pretty much," Consuela nodded. "He's the one paying for my degree."

The waiter returned to the table and put down two glasses. He opened the bottle and let Consuela taste the wine before pouring it.

"So…" Samuel said after he'd sipped the wine. "Tell me about your research project. You mentioned you had a few ideas."

"The project," Consuela rolled her eyes and drank her wine. "Would you mind if we talked about something else for a while? It's been a long week, and it's Friday…"

"Okay," Samuel said slowly, staring at her and deciding how to respond.

"What?" Consuela said, returning his stare. "What is it?"

"Well," Samuel began, hesitant at first. "I'm wondering whether you have any intention of talking about the research project tonight?"

"What do you mean?"

"This meeting—you said you wanted to talk about your project, but I think maybe that was all just a ruse? A pretense?"

"Of course not."

"I think it was," Samuel continued, slugging deeply on his wine to fortify himself. "You know a friend of mine, Dr Shetty? Dr Arjun Shetty?"

"Of course. He was in charge of the first-year biology students last year."

"You know he's left our faculty here in London? He moved to Edinburgh University over the summer."

"I did hear he'd moved."

"You know why he moved?"

"I expect it was a promotion," Consuela said.

"No, it most certainly wasn't. A demotion more like. He moved to get away from you—under orders from his wife."

"From me? Whatever for?"

"Come on Consuela… I think you know why."

"Really, I don't know what you're talking about."

"You don't think the fact you were having an affair with him had anything to do with it?"

"Rubbish!" Consuela looked shocked at the accusation. "Who told you that?"

"He did, Arjun himself."

"It's not true."

"Please…" Samuel looked at Consuela and softened his tone. "Arjun told me everything. You're an attractive woman, he's a middle-aged professor. You made a play for him, and he folded like a sheet."

"Like a sheet?" Consuela giggled. "I never heard that expression before."

"You know what I mean. He was flattered and it didn't take much to turn his eye."

"It's all rubbish. Arjun… Dr Shetty told you this? He has a very fertile imagination. I know him, of course, but not like that… We certainly weren't having an affair."

"There's no use denying it. His wife found out and caused a huge fuss. She wanted a divorce. It was a terrible mess. Not that you'd know about any of that. It happened during the summer."

"I'm sorry to hear that…"

"His wife only agreed to stay with him if they moved. So Arjun called in all his favours. He found an opening in Edinburgh."

"Like I said, I…"

"Don't bother…" Samuel held up his hand and shook his

head. "Arjun's a good friend of mine. He told me about you long before his wife found out. He pointed you out to me last term, but it was only when I saw you in my lecture that I understood how the situation came about. Arjun's a very serious man, an excellent scholar, not prone to distraction. But you're… You're just incredibly flirtatious. I can see how easily you could turn a man's head."

"But why would I?" Consuela pleaded.

"Because you're ambitious. I don't know if you're clever or not. But my guess is that you don't want to take any chances. You had an affair with Arjun to help with your grades. Don't worry, I checked. Three As and one B after your first year. That's very impressive."

"You think I didn't earn those grades?"

"I'm sure you earned them, but perhaps not in the right way. I think you had Arjun twisted round your little finger and he helped you," Samuel knocked back the rest of his wine. "But there's a big cost to your methods. You've done huge damage to Arjun's career. You've broken his marriage, hopefully not beyond repair. Arjun told me you even stole from him. You took money from his wallet, but he turned a blind eye because…"

"Okay, okay," Consuela looked as though she might cry. "I did have an affair with him. I just wanted some help. You don't know how important this is to me."

"What is?"

"My degree. I'm under so much pressure from my family, from my father. The expectation is huge."

"Everyone's under pressure, you know…"

"Yes, but not like me," Consuela pleaded. "My father studied biology. He got a first from Imperial, then he got his masters. If I get anything less, the disappointment…"

"So this is all about your father?"

"No… not entirely. I do want to take over the business. But his standards are so high."

"Whereas yours are so low?" Samuel shook his head. "Sleeping with your lecturer to secure your grades…"

"I don't regret it," Consuela looked at him proudly.

"Evidently not, because you're trying to do the same thing all over again. I'm not an attractive man, I know that. But the way you behave in my lectures… I don't know, you'd think I was a rock star."

"I like your lectures."

"Maybe you do, but there's more to it than that isn't there?"

Consuela looked down at the table and said nothing.

"I mean look at us here. Look at you, dolled up to the nines in your skimpy dress, inviting me out for drinks. You're doing the same thing all over again."

"I'm sorry."

"Doesn't any of this bother you? Wouldn't you rather get the grades on merit, on the back of your own efforts?"

"I do work hard, very hard. I study harder than anyone. I just don't know if I'm good enough to get a first."

"And it doesn't bother you, sleeping your way to the top, so to speak? You don't feel guilty?"

"The end justifies the means."

"I see," Samuel said, rubbing his chin with his hand. "How apt. Here we are drinking in Bentham's—the master of utilitarianism—and you spout consequentialist ethics at me."

"What will you do?" Consuela asked. "You won't report me will you?"

"I've thought about it a lot. What you've done is cheating. It isn't fair. It's not right to break up families to further your personal ambitions. It's not fair to hurt people like Arjun's wife…"

"I'm very sorry about that. She wasn't supposed to know. I ended it with Arjun before the summer. I don't know how she found out."

"Well she did."

"Please don't report me."

"You've caused Arjun a lifetime of regret," Samuel sighed. "The sad part is that if he'd been principled and turned you down, he'd have spent the rest of his time regretting that decision too, that he passed up something he really desired. You put him in a lose/lose situation."

"That was never my intention."

"The thing is," Samuel said, looking around the room. The guarded stares from other men in the bar were quite clear, no matter how subtle they tried to be. They desired Consuela. And the more they drank, the more they felt they could have her. But could they? Perhaps she was more disciplined than that. Perhaps she only chose those who were useful to her. "The thing is that I don't have a family. I'm not married."

"What?" Consuela looked up and stared at the professor. "I don't understand?"

"I'm in a different position to Arjun, so the balance of regret is much more one-sided."

"Are you…" Consuela looked confused. "So you're saying…"

"What I'm saying is that I'd like a girlfriend. I find you attractive. And if you want help getting a first, then I can do that."

"Really? You'd help me?"

"But if we do this, let's have all our cards on the table. No deceit between us. You know what I want. I know what you want. It's all above board."

"What do you mean?"

"I mean you don't have to pretend I'm a rockstar. In fact, it would be much better if you feigned indifference towards me, like every other student. But once a week we can get together, maybe after my lecture. We can have a drink or two, and… well, you can deliver on your side of the arrangement."

"What about your side of the deal?"

"I can look after that."

"You'll help me get a first? Get the right grades?"

"Yes," Samuel nodded.

Consuela smiled at him and lifted her glass. "Deal."

The following morning, Samuel woke late. The morning light outside the window in his bedroom was cold and grey. He rolled over and saw that Consuela was gone. It was just as well, he thought. There was no use pretending their relationship was anything other than a business deal. He reached for the watch on his bedside table to check the time, but the watch was gone too.

11

NOVEMBER: BETTER NEVER THAN LATE

Walter Wick lay under his covers enjoying the warmth that had built up after a night's sleep. The door to his bathroom was open and he could hear his girlfriend taking a shower. Steam wafted into the cold air of the bedroom and strengthened Walter's determination to stay in bed. On mornings like this he wished he was a bear and could hibernate for the next four months. Once he was up and ready, he enjoyed the cold. But forcing himself each morning to transition from a warm duvet to a chill morning was always a dismal prospect.

"You'll be late," Consuela said, walking into the bedroom, wrapped in towels.

"No I won't."

"It's 9.00am already."

"If I turned up at 9.30am, that would be late," Walter said, picking up his watch and looking at the time. "But if I turn up at 11.00am, that's not late at all. That's me having already had an appointment."

"Pretending to have had an appointment… Do you mind if your staff are late?"

"Of course."

"But it's okay for you?"

"I'm an artist, I create things. Punctuality doesn't help the creative process," Walter put the watch down and closed his eyes. He worked as the creative director for Bogard Black, an advertising agency in Soho. He'd been in the industry for thirty years. "You know what Oscar Wilde said about punctuality? He said 'punctuality is the thief of time'."

"I don't know why I gave you that watch…"

"Because you adore me," Walter sat up and pulled Consuela down onto the bed and kissed her. "Are you coming to the exhibition tonight?"

"You know I can't."

"You're serious? You'd rather have extra tuition with your professor than meet Clive Block?"

"It's boring, I know," Consuela said.

"Clive's one of Britain's greatest living artists."

"I'd love to, but Professor Mason is being so generous with his time. I can't let him down."

"Such a conscientious student," Walter sighed and slumped back onto the bed. "You're young, you're supposed to be enjoying life. You should be setting an example to an old fart like me, keeping me young too."

"Poor old man," Consuela said, stroking his face. She stood and finished dressing herself. "I'll see you on Saturday. You can tell me all about it."

Later that evening, Walter made his way to The Greenleaf Gallery in St John's Wood. The day had turned dark, and the gallery windows were spilling light onto the pavement. A crowd inside were drinking champagne and talking and looking at the paintings. Walter pushed open the door and a woman at the entrance welcomed him and took his coat.

"Walter, so glad you could make it," the gallery owner, a small man in glasses and a suit, rushed over to greet him. "Your paintings are in the back gallery if you want to check up on them."

"I'm sure you've looked after them perfectly," Walter

said. He owned two paintings by Clive Block. Usually they hung on the walls of his study at home, in pride of place above his desk. But for today, and for the next month, the gallery had asked to borrow them as part of the exhibition.

"We've hung them with the rest of Clive's earlier work. This room is all his new stuff."

"So I see."

"It works very nicely, the old and the new. There's a real sense of evolution."

"How has the new work been received?"

"We've sold two already this evening." The gallery owner's eyes gleamed with venal excitement.

"I'd better take a look then," Walter said, feeling irritated by the man.

"Do," the gallery owner bowed and gestured towards the paintings. "Clive's here somewhere. I'll ask him to come over."

Walter glanced around the room. Clive's new work looked similar in style to his earlier paintings. He used oils daubed onto canvasses so thickly that the surface of the paintings became deeply uneven, making them shimmer with texture and movement and reflected light. But while the surfaces of the paintings were uneven, the brush strokes themselves were refined and precise, with the paint built up tirelessly, layer upon layer.

Clive's early works had all been self-portraits rendered in stunning detail despite the impasto style of the paintwork. The new paintings in the front gallery showed a different theme. They were all of dancers. Walter studied the first, a nightclub scene. The background was a dance floor full of energy and movement, but with all the figures semi-shrouded in dry-ice smoke lit by strobe lighting, or else cloaked in umbrous anonymity. Only in one part of the painting did the smoke and darkness give way to reveal a single dancer in absolute clarity. It was a young woman, perhaps twenty-five years old, dressed in a ballerina's tutu and pink ballet slippers. She was caught in mid-air, but rather than executing a traditional ballet move, her legs were flying wildly and her arms were punching the air. Her expression was exuberant and militant and full of abandon.

"Quite something isn't it?" the gallery owner glided alongside Walter. "Can I introduce you to Clive?"

"Of course," Walter said turning and finding the artist behind him. Clive was tall, with long, dirty blond hair. He looked more like a surfer than an artist. Walter held out his hand. "We met once before, at your first exhibition."

"Yes, I remember," Clive shook Walter's hand. "You bought a painting didn't you?"

"Two paintings. They're here today, in the back."

"It's kind of you to lend them to us."

"It's a pleasure, I'm a big fan." Walter was surprised at the politeness of the artist. His paintings showed such youthful angst. "This one here is fantastic," Walter said, "I love the composition. It reminds me a little of Degas."

"Because she's a ballerina?" Clive asked.

"Yes, but also because it's filled with people, and yet your eye is drawn to just one figure."

"Don't you love the expression on her face?" the gallery owner cut in. "So passionate, so much energy… it's so Clive Block."

"I do like it. And the sense of movement too."

"It's palpable isn't it?" the gallery owner agreed. "The picture writhes before your eyes."

"That was the intention," Clive forced a smile to hide his embarrassment.

"Why dancers?" Walter asked, looking across at some of the other pictures.

"Because of the movement. I like to paint a single moment in time, but then show that moment so full of motion that your brain just carries it forward."

"Like in your self portraits," Walter nodded.

"And dancing as a form of self-expression…" Clive searched for the right words, "it's so raw, so immediate. It expresses what's at the centre of your soul."

"Not necessarily if you're a ballet dancer…"

"That's why she's at a rave. She's been unshackled."

"You've liberated her?"

"I tried to."

"You succeeded." Walter took a glass of champagne from a passing waiter.

"I'm happy you like it," Clive said.

"Maybe you should buy it," the gallery owner winked.

Walter peered at the label beside the picture where the price was listed as £36,000. At Clive's first exhibition, Walter had paid £14,000 for two pictures.

"I see your prices have gone up."

"It's the demand," the gallery owner shrugged. "Clive's widely known these days. One of his self-portraits sold at auction the other day for £43,000."

Walter spent the next half an hour looking at the rest of the new paintings, before moving into the back of the gallery to look at Clive's earlier work. The gallery owner was right, Walter realised. The paintings here were angrier and more iconoclastic. All were self-portraits, and all showed Clive in an act of violence, not against other people, but against art itself.

The two paintings that Walter owned were hung side-by-side. The canvases were large—five feet by six feet—and covered in the same textured painting style as the newer work. The first painting showed Clive, bare-chested, with blue overalls tied around his waist, facing a picture on a wall. The picture was Marcel Duchamp's "Nude Descending a Staircase No 2", a futurist-style depiction of a person walking downstairs, with the motion captured as a series of multiple blurred, abstract positions. It was one of Duchamp's most famous pictures, yet in the self-portrait Clive was throwing a pot of red paint onto it. Clive had depicted his own face contorted with hatred, and his muscles tense with determination. The moment frozen in time was just as the red paint was leaving the pot, on course to hit the Duchamp hanging on the wall.

The second painting showed Clive from behind and slightly to the left, his body entirely naked. This time, the artwork in the painting was Jackson Pollock's "No 5", arguably his most famous piece of abstract expressionism. The artwork was lying flat on the floor, a mass of yellow and brown paint splats and dribbles that together looked like straw on a stable floor. Clive was standing on top of the Pollock, his back arched, his face pointing towards the ceiling, and he was urinating onto the painting beneath his feet. Though the painting didn't show Clive's face, the tension in his body spoke of a thrusting effort to pee as high and as hard as he could onto the painting below. Walter loved the painting for many reasons, not least for the irony that Pollock had himself painted in a similar way, by laying sheets of fibreboard on the floor and then dripping and flicking and splashing paint onto them.

Walter himself wasn't an artist in a true sense, not like Clive Block. Walter didn't draw or paint or sculpt. As the creative director of Bogard Black, his creativity was all about bringing brands and companies to life, and persuading customers to buy more products. His job was to make people feel fit and sporty when they wore certain types of trainers, or to feel secure putting their money into certain banks, or to think themselves refined buying certain brands of coffee.

But in the presence of his two Clive Blocks, Walter saw a deeper value in his work. He created feature films that told a story in thirty seconds. He wrote radio plays that lasted only twenty seconds but which still made an audience laugh out loud. He drafted beautiful posters, created imaginative characters and cartoons, and dreamt up engaging experiences. On one level they were just advertisements and marketing, but on another they were also creative and inventive and rich in emotional content that touched people.

Walter had come to think of his two Clive Block paintings as the touchstone of his creativity. Walter was 50 years old, and advertising was a young man's game. But having the Blocks kept him in touch with his latent youth. They inspired him. They reminded him of what it felt like to be twenty again. He'd won five pencil awards from D&AD over the past six years, and the Blocks were a big part of his success. Walter was convinced of it.

Next to Walter's two paintings in the gallery were other pictures from Clive's series of self portraits. Walter had seen many of them before, at the artist's first exhibition seven years earlier. But there was one that he hadn't seen. In a far corner, Walter spotted a portrait where the artwork being attacked by Clive was Roy Lichtenstein's 1963 cartoon painting "Whaam!", with a US fighter jet depicted in comic-strip style firing its machine guns at an enemy plane. In this picture, Clive had once again painted himself full of fury and violence and motion. He was caught swinging an axe, the sort used to fell trees, with the moment in the picture being just fractions of a second before the axe tore into the Lichtenstein.

Walter stood in front of the picture, stunned by the passion in the painting. It wasn't just the expression on the artist's face, it was the anger in his knuckles that gripped the axe handle, the taut resolve of the muscles in his arms and shoulders, the commitment to violence in the full-bodied twist of his hips. And just as in Clive's other paintings, this one had a sense of motion that burst from the canvas. It wasn't a single moment, it was the whole action, the full sweep of the swing from start to crunching completion.

Walter checked the label on the wall. Just as he feared, the painting was only in the exhibition on loan. It belonged to somebody called Park Kook-hyun. A Korean, Walter guessed. Clive really had hit the big time, it seemed, with an international following and paintings selling for nearly £50,000. It was inevitable, Walter thought, but also saddening. Looking at the painting, he felt a deep yearning to own it. The picture would go so perfectly with the two that he already owned. Together, they'd form a trio of muses, a triptych in honour of free-thinking and rebellion and iconoclasm and rejection of the accepted.

Walter looked at the other portraits and, though they were good, none were as fine as the two that he owned, and the third that he didn't. Walter felt a deep craving to hang all three together. How wonderful it would be, he thought, to work in the company of all three, and to draw inspiration from their collective message. He considered asking the gallery owner to put him in touch with the Korean owner, but he realised it would be futile. Even if the Korean was willing to sell, Walter didn't have £50,000 to spare. He didn't have any spare cash at present.

As the exhibition drew to a close, Walter visited the loo at the back of the gallery, and it was then that he was struck with an idea. It began as just a scrap of a notion. One of the stalls in the loo had a window set high in the wall, close to the ceiling. Walter stood on the loo seat and reached up. The window opened, and was wide enough to crawl through. Perhaps he could steal the picture? Walter smiled at the thought. It was a wild notion, and anyway, the picture wouldn't fit back through the window. He dismissed the idea.

Outside the loo, though, Walter noticed a back door to the gallery. He flicked the latch, turned the handle, and pulled it open. Outside, the gallery backed onto a narrow lane. Weeds grew in the gutters, a pile of bricks was stacked a little further down. The lane seemed dark and disused. Walter ducked back in and closed the door. Instinctively he wiped the handle clean with the sleeve of his jacket.

Thoughts raced through his mind. What if a burglar came in through the window, and then out through the back door? That way they could certainly get the picture out undamaged. Walter ducked back into the loo. He reached up and unlatched the window with the sleeve of his shirt, leaving the window shut, but not locked. He pulled a pen from his jacket pocket and a business card and drew a sketch of the layout of the loo. Out in the gallery, he drew a second plan of the exhibition room, the back door, and the connecting corridors and furniture. A plan began to form in his head.

Four days later, he called up Lester Price and arranged to meet him in a pub in Enfield after work. Lester worked as a decorator, and Walter had used him a few times, to re-paint his kitchen, to put up shelves, and to clean his gutters. Walter knew him because his mother worked as a nurse who cared for

Walter's father.

"Lester, how are you?" Walter found him standing at the bar with a pint of lager.

"Good," he nodded, shaking Walter's hand. Lester was a man of few words, and few friends. Walter found him pleasant, and he worked hard, but importantly he was also shy and awkward in social situations. And he had a soft spot for Walter. He was in his mid-thirties, fifteen years younger than Walter, and gave the impression of respecting whatever Walter said. All of which made him suitable for the job.

"How's business?"

"Okay," Lester nodded.

"Got a lot of work on?"

"Some. I could use a bit more."

"I might have something for you."

"What's that?"

"Let me get a drink first, and another for you."

Walter ordered and took Lester to a corner table that was private.

"New watch is it?" Lester asked, nodding at Walter's wrist.

"Consuela gave it to me."

"The Spanish bird?"

"Yes."

"Looks expensive."

"It was a present," Walter said, looking at the watch briefly, then waving the matter away. "So this job, it's a bit unusual. I have to trust you that you won't say a word about it."

"Why's that?"

"It's not exactly legal."

"Dangerous is it?"

"Only if we get caught. Which we won't."

"What is it?"

"Do I have your word? You won't say anything to anyone about it? Whether you do it or not, you have to promise me you'll keep quiet."

"Okay," Lester nodded.

"You can't tell your mother, or anyone."

"Okay."

"I want you to help me steal something, a painting."

"Where is it?"

"In an art gallery."

"Like the Mona Lisa or something?"

"No, nothing like that. You won't even know the artist. It's not famous or valuable. Nobody will care if we take it."

"Then why do you want it?"

"It's for a friend of mine," Walter lied. "I owe him a favour, a big favour. He helped me out once before, and now he's asked me to help him."

"To pay him back?"

"Exactly."

"Can't you just buy the painting?"

"It's not for sale, that's the problem. But it should be easy to steal. We can pretty much walk in, take it and walk out."

"Why do you need me then?"

"First of all, I need someone with a van. The painting's too big to fit in a car, but it'll fit in your van. Plus, it's a two-man job. There's a little alley that runs behind the gallery. We drive your van into the alley, then climb in through a bathroom window—it's small and difficult for me to get through it, but you could do it. Once you're in, you can unlock the backdoor and bring the picture out. It's very simple."

"Don't they have security alarms and video cameras?"

"There's nothing like that, I've checked."

"What about those laser beams, the ones that detect movement?"

"No," Walter laughed. "It's a tiny gallery. They don't have anything sophisticated. It's very simple."

"What if someone sees us?"

"They won't. The lane behind the gallery is completely disused. There aren't even street lights. The whole job would take two or three minutes. In and out. There's no chance of anyone seeing us."

"Will anyone be inside the gallery? Like guards?"

"No, we'd do it at night. The place would be empty."

"It doesn't sound right. Why doesn't your friend do it himself?"

"He's an old man," Walter expanded on his earlier lie. "He isn't up to it."

"I don't know," Lester shook his head.

"I'll pay you, of course, and make it worth your while."

"How much?"

"How about a grand?"

"A grand? Pounds?" Lester's eyes lit up, then narrowed. "It must be dangerous if you're paying that much."

"No, really it isn't. I tell you what. I'll drive you to the alley. You can see for yourself. Take a look at the lane, see the window you have to climb through. Then make up your mind."

When they'd finished their drinks, Walter drove Lester to St John's Wood in his MG. It was 9.00pm when they arrived and the gallery had shut for the night. The lane was dark and empty, just as Walter knew it would be.

"There's the window," he said, pointing it out to Lester. "I'll have to give you a boost, or I suppose you could climb up on the bonnet of your van."

"You want me to smash the window?"

"No, it's unlocked. You just have to pull it open. On the other side it's a toilet. You climb in, grab the picture off the wall, and come out through the back door, over there. We put the painting in your van and away we go."

"How will I know where to find it, the painting?"

"I'll draw you a map. Honestly, it's very easy. You'll be inside for a minute, maybe two at the most. The painting is really close to the toilet. You won't get lost."

"I don't think I can do it," Lester shook his head. "I'd feel so nervous. I feel nervous just thinking about it."

"Look around you. It's completely dark. Nobody in their right mind would walk down here at night. There's no way to get caught."

"What about fingerprints?"

"We'll use gloves."

"Or footprints?"

"We'll tie plastic bags over our shoes. Just shopping bags will do."

"I don't think…"

"How about I give you more money?" Walter said. "I know what. How about I give you my watch?"

"It was a present wasn't it?"

"Consuela won't mind. I don't know how much it's worth, but probably a couple of grand. I'll give you a thousand pounds and my watch. How about that?"

A week later, everything was agreed and the date was set for Thursday night. Walter would take a taxi to a street nearby the gallery, then walk the last part and meet Lester by his van at 2.00am in the alley. Walter had organised gloves and a torch and bags for their shoes. He'd also purchased balaclavas, not just to hide their faces, but to prevent any hair from falling onto the crime scene. All of this was now stashed in Lester's van. Earlier in the week, Walter had drawn a detailed map of the inside of the gallery and drilled Lester until he knew it perfectly. And he'd printed off a picture of Lichtenstein's "Whaam!" and described in detail what the painting looked like. Everything was set.

By the time Thursday evening arrived, Walter felt more nervous than he had expected. His bowels kept prompting him to visit the loo, as if preparing him for danger ahead. Walter opened a bottle of wine to quell his butterflies and watched television as he waited.

At 4.00am, Walter woke suddenly. Somebody was ringing his doorbell. He looked at his watch and saw the time. Panic set in. He'd missed the rendezvous with Lester. He jumped up, turned off the television, and paced the room, his mind both instantly awake, but also confused and unfocused. Shit, shit, shit, he kept saying to himself. The doorbell rang again, longer this time.

Walter crept up to the door and peered through the

viewfinder. He expected to see the police. Lester had been caught. He'd told them everything and now the police had come to question him. Walter's heart was pounding in his chest. But when he looked through the viewfinder, he saw Lester on the step outside, a balaclava rolled up on his head so that it looked like a black hat. Walter opened the door cautiously.

"What happened?" Lester asked.

"Are you alone?" Walter peered over Lester's shoulder.

"Yes."

"Come in, quickly."

"Why didn't you come? I waited for an hour."

"I'm so sorry," Walter said closing the door. "I fell asleep. I had a couple of glasses of wine and then fell asleep on the sofa. I feel terrible. I'm so sorry."

"That's all? You just fell asleep?"

"That's all."

"Nothing serious then?"

"It's been such a waste of your time. I really can't apologise enough."

"No, it's okay. I got the picture."

"What…"

"It's outside in the van."

"You went ahead anyway?" Walter's heart started pounding again. He'd wanted to be there to make sure everything was done properly. What if Lester had made a mistake, or left some sort of evidence?

"I waited for an hour, but the lane was so dead. There wasn't nothing moving that whole hour. So I figured, why not do it anyway?"

"Where's your van?"

"Out on the street."

"Can you move it? Back it up the garage at the side of the house. We'll get the painting out. Go out the back door."

Lester went out and did as he was instructed. Walter opened the garage doors. His MG was parked inside, but there was plenty of space to store the picture. Lester parked the van, opened the doors and lifted out the painting. He carried it into the garage and placed it on the floor at the back.

"Here's the torch if you want to check it," Lester said. Walter closed the garage doors and flicked on the torch. His face broke into a smile. There it was. The painting he had craved so deeply, now in his home, ready to be hung alongside his other two Clive Blocks as soon as they were returned from the gallery.

"Lester, you're a bloody genius." Walter wrapped his arms around his accomplice. "Come inside. Let's have a coffee, or a drink or something."

In the kitchen, Walter counted out a thousand pounds onto the table. He unstrapped his watch and placed it on top of the money and pushed the pile over to Lester.

"Well deserved," he said. "So you're sure nobody saw you?"

"There wasn't a soul around," Lester said, taking the money and holding up the watch to examine it more closely.

"And you wore the gloves, and the bags on your shoes?"

"Just as you said."

"So there's absolutely no chance you left anything behind? No clues, nothing dropped. Just straight in and out."

"They won't find nothing," Lester said.

"Good." Walter stood and reached for a bottle of whiskey.

"Nothing but a burnt-out shell."

"What?" Walter said, almost dropping the bottle. "What do you mean?"

"I didn't leave nothing to chance."

"I don't understand?"

"I thought to myself this afternoon, you can't be too careful can you? So I took a can of petrol with me and torched the place."

"You set fire to the gallery?"

"Like I said, they won't find nothing. They won't even know a painting was taken."

12

DECEMBER: MEMORY LANE

Conrad Sands stood on the street outside his new house in Holland Park. A taxi engine coughed and spluttered clouds of blue exhaust into the frigid midday air in front of him as the passengers inside paid their fare. Conrad held open the door as a man stepped down onto the pavement followed by a woman. They looked smart. The man wore a blue suit, the woman a long black overcoat and scarf. She had striking red hair.

Inside the taxi, a hint of perfume hung in the air. Conrad sniffed at it as he sat back in his seat. He recognised the scent. He'd known a woman long ago who had once worn the same fragrance. Who was the woman? The memory of her lay locked deep in his mind, just beyond the reach of his consciousness. Conrad sniffed harder, trying to catch more of the scent, but it was fading rapidly, and like a sneeze that evaporates before it erupts, Conrad lost hold of the memory without ever recalling it. He felt frustrated at the loss. The memory had seemed like a pleasant one and he wished he'd been able to resurrect it.

Conrad turned in his seat and watched the couple walking down the street, arm-in-arm, she resting her head on his shoulder, her rich red hair splayed across his jacket. The woman held out her hand as she walked, seemingly admiring a ring on her finger, and Conrad wondered if the two of them had recently become engaged.

"Where to?" the driver asked.

"Dean Street, in Soho," Conrad replied. "There's a place called 'The Eleventh Hour'. Do you know it?"

"The restaurant?"

"Yes."

The taxi pulled out onto Bayswater Road and made its way towards Marble Arch, then down Oxford Street. Christmas decorations filled the shop windows and hung from lampposts across the street. Shoppers in coats and hats moved briskly through the holly- and tinsel-strewn doorways of department stores and arcades.

On Regent Street, the taxi crawled past Hamleys toy store and Conrad watched short-tempered parents trying to marshal their excited children. A strait-laced looking man emerged from the shop with his wife and their daughter. He was clutching a receipt and studying it closely through screwed up eyes. The daughter, perhaps ten years old, was clutching a Hamleys shopping bag and peeking into it as they walked, her eyes alive with pleasure. Conrad found himself smiling, enjoying her delight vicariously at the early Christmas treasure in her bag. But as he watched, he saw a glove slip from her coat pocket and fall softly to the pavement. Neither she nor her parents saw it fall, and all of them continued walking, oblivious to the loss.

The pleasure that Conrad had felt moments earlier slipped into a familiar melancholy as memories bubbled up of many of his own Christmases—recollections of disappointment and anti-climax, of bright promises only partially delivered. Conrad wanted to stop the taxi and retrieve the glove for the girl, but it was too late, the traffic had moved on.

As the taxi reached Piccadilly Circus, the throngs of shoppers grew thicker, and slowed Conrad's progress as they streamed across the road. The taxi driver honked his horn to hurry the pedestrians along and drew an acid look from a Chinese woman. She stopped in the middle of the road and glared at the driver. With her were two young girls and another woman—Asian, but not Chinese. It was a picture immediately familiar to Conrad from his days living in Hong Kong. A haughty Chinese tai tai on a shopping trip, dressed in the finest clothes and talking into a mobile phone, as her children were shepherded along behind her by a Filipina amah.

The taxi pulled into Shaftesbury Avenue and then into Dean Street and deposited Conrad outside the restaurant. He pushed through the glass doors and entered a cavernous modern space of brushed steel and minimalist wooden benches. The place looked cold, but thick currents of hot air greeted those walking in off the street. Conrad was early and took a stool at the bar while he waited.

He ordered a beer and while it was being poured, he unbuckled his watch and held it in his hands, turning it over and over. It was the watch that Mariana had given him more than twenty years earlier. He was certain of it. The style and brand were identical—a Breitling chronometer, built from rose-coloured gold. The inscription on the back was the same too: "May your brief candle shine brightly." The watch even had the extra hole in the strap that Mariana had punched through the leather to make it fit her wrist. Conrad had no doubt it was Mariana's watch. But how had it come into the possession of his decorator?

After buying his house in Holland Park, Conrad had hired a painter, Lester Price, to help fix it up. Lester had left the watch in the kitchen one day. Conrad had noticed it lying on the side and had taken a closer look. Lester told him another client had given him the watch as payment for a job, and that he planned to sell it. Conrad had asked who the client was, but the name meant nothing to him—it wasn't Mariana anyway. Conrad had made Lester an offer, eventually agreeing a price of three thousand pounds.

It was expensive, but Conrad couldn't bear to leave the watch in the hands of a stranger. It belonged on the wrist of

Mariana, and if not, then on his own. Seeing it in Lester's possession had made Conrad sad. He'd returned the watch to Mariana a year earlier. How had it strayed so far from her? Lester had simply shrugged when Conrad had asked him if he knew anything more about the watch.

Conrad turned it back and forth in his fingers, feeling the warmth and smoothness of the metal casing. He wondered if he should contact Mariana again. He could tell her he had found her watch. Nearly twelve months had passed since he'd last seen her, sitting at the bar of a restaurant in Notting Hill. Back in January, the time hadn't been right to talk to her, but Conrad had moved on since then. He had new purpose now—a purpose partly inspired by Mariana.

For the first three months of the year he hadn't done much at all. He'd visited museums and read books and reconnected with old friends, searching for inspiration for what to do next with his life. But nothing had excited him. He had felt tired and listless.

Then, in April, he'd met an old friend of his from Singapore—an Indian fund manager called Vishrut. Over dinner, Vishrut had complained about the architectural decay in his native Bombay. His old school—a Victorian confection of Doric columns, crenellations and Gothic arched windows set around a formal quadrangle—was typical. The school had been set up in 1885, but after operating for 118 years in south Bombay, the school had run out of money in 2003.

Vishrut had described how the building's elegant balconies and stone balustrades were collapsing into rubble. The site was a wreck of rusting wires and broken air-conditioners, smashed windows and crumbling walls where trees had taken root in the cracks.

"Bombay's losing its memory," Vishrut had said. "Buildings like that inspire you. As a student, the architecture gives you a sense of possibility and wonder. And now it's disappearing."

"Why don't they restore it?" Conrad had asked.

"Too expensive," he'd shrugged. "It's much cheaper to

knock down the old and build anew. But that's what I mean about memory—cities in India are losing their past."

Conrad had thought about their conversation afterwards and realised he felt the same way as Vishrut. During his fifteen years working in Asia, Conrad had witnessed first-hand the development in countries like China. Whole cities now existed where the oldest building was less than twenty years old. Any kind of architectural heritage had been flattened and destroyed under the bulldozers of modernisation.

Four months later, in August, Conrad had launched The Cinderella Foundation. Its aim was to preserve the world's architectural heritage—but not in rich countries, only in poor ones. The philosophy was simple: architecture is important. It provides the context to people's lives. It tells them where they've come from. It shapes their identity. If people lose their old buildings, they lose their culture, their history, their sense of who they are.

The Cinderella Foundation was a market place where restoration projects in poor countries could find money and expertise from donors and companies that wanted to help. The name of the foundation alluded to the poor sister in the Cinderella fairy tale, who was transformed after years of neglect to reveal her true beauty.

Ever since its launch, Conrad had worked tirelessly getting the project off the ground. So far, the exchange had funded four projects, including Vishrut's old school in Bombay. Conrad had persuaded Vishrut, and a group of fellow investors, to buy the building for US$27m from the charity that owned the old school. The proceeds of the sale would be administered as a scholarship fund, helping a new generation of Indian children to attend schools and universities. Meanwhile, the new owners of the old school would renovate the buildings and convert them into modern offices built around a courtyard of shops and restaurants. It would no longer be a school, but Bombay would get to keep an architectural landmark.

Conrad strapped the watch back onto his wrist and sipped

his beer. Across the room, a chef strode out of the open-plan kitchen with a pair of secateurs in his hand. Along one of the walls stood a sideboard lined with plants. Conrad guessed they were herbs, for the chef went along the row of plants snipping off sprigs and leaves and gathering the cuttings in his hand.

The tables in the restaurant were starting to fill with lunchtime diners. In one corner, Conrad's eye was drawn to a table of three men. One of them, the youngest of the three, was almost certainly a journalist, for he held a reporter's notebook in his hand and occasionally wrote in it as the others spoke. His interview subjects struck Conrad as an unusual combination. One was dressed in a drab gray suit and looked like an accountant or a banker. The other gave the impression of a tropical bird. His hair was gelled up like an elaborate crest plumage, and he wore a bright orange shirt beneath a purple velvet jacket. Conrad wondered who the two interviewees could be and what they were talking about.

Outside on the pavement, people strode past the restaurant, rushing to meetings and appointments, or hurrying just to get out of the cold. A woman wrapped in a scarf lifted her head momentarily as she crossed the street and her features reminded Conrad of someone. Who was it? Mariana? Yes, that was who she looked like. It wasn't her, Conrad told himself, but for just an instant she had reminded him of her. At least, she reminded him of Mariana as she had looked sitting on her barstool back in January when Conrad had been too insecure to say hello.

A man stopped to read the menu displayed outside the restaurant. He was small and slight, with thinning hair and looked under-dressed for the weather. He wore a green tweed jacket, with brown patches at the elbows, and a brown scarf. Conrad watched him and realised that he bore a strong similarity to one of the mathematics teachers at his secondary school, Mr Mennon. The resemblance was striking—the sunken eyes and hollow cheeks, the sense of academic detachment from the world around him, almost a deliberate detachment, as if the world was a place to be avoided.

How odd, Conrad thought, that his memory of Mr Mennon should come back to him with such sharp definition. Conrad hadn't thought about him in more than twenty years. That memory had lain dormant without any reference or recall for more than two decades, and yet here it was, open once again, quite clear in his mind. Where did these memories live, he wondered, that lay so dormant and untouched for so long, and yet so sharp when recalled?

A woman with two teenage sons stopped beside the man to look at the menu board, displacing him and causing him to scurry away. After a minute of conversation, the woman and her sons entered the restaurant and were directed to a table. The elder of her two sons was talking into a mobile phone, the younger one—perhaps fourteen or fifteen—looked bored and embarrassed to be with his mother.

Conrad turned his gaze back to the bar and drank more of his beer. The barman was opening a tin of beef consommé and pouring it into a cocktail shaker, along with vodka, lemon juice, Tabasco and seasoning. Conrad knew the drink—a bullshot. His father had drunk them on weekends during the winters when Conrad was a child. He'd said they fortified him and kept him warm on cold days. Conrad had never liked them himself, but the smell—the odour of thick meatiness—took him back to the kitchen of his parents' cottage outside St Austell, with its stout white walls and low ceilings and the fierce winds outside. Both his parents were dead now, and the cottage had been sold long ago. Conrad tilted his beer towards the bullshot in silent tribute to them.

The noise in the restaurant was growing louder as lunchtime conversation took hold. Conrad listened to the chatter, trying to pick out individual voices and conversations, but the words were mixed too thoroughly to identify the ingredients. Underneath it all, though, he heard music. He listened harder until he recognised it: Handel's Messiah. Perfect for Christmas, Conrad thought. He'd heard it performed live many times, but none had compared to the first time, a performance in St Paul's Cathedral during the winter of 1995.

Or was it 1994? Conrad had been reluctant to attend, only going to keep his girlfriend at the time happy. But hearing the 60-strong choir and the orchestra and the power of the soloists as their voices soared and resonated around the cathedral had touched something deep within him. It had been a meditative experience, a path to a deeper place within himself.

The door of the restaurant pushed open and a woman walked in and took a stool at the other end of the bar to Conrad. He watched her absently as she took off her coat and laid it on the bar. She ordered a glass of wine and then turned on her stool to watch the rest of the room, just as Conrad had been doing.

Conrad looked at her face and realised that she had been in an accident at some stage in her life. The skin was badly burnt and scalded. Parts of her cheek and forehead were stretched and taut with scars that looked like melted plastic. Other parts were discoloured with brown streaks and stains. It was difficult to know how old she was, but from the "better" side of her face, where the scars were less serious, he guessed she was in her early forties.

Conrad looked at her and wondered what it must be like to undergo an accident like that, to be scarred for life, branded forever thanks to just a single moment. It seemed impossible that an incident that had doubtless lasted just a few seconds could leave such an indelible mark on a lifetime of years.

And as Conrad thought about it, he was struck by an impression of all humans as being deeply scarred—not physically, but psychologically, emotionally. Every experience left its mark, sometimes a small nick, sometimes a blemish, occasionally a giant disfigurement. Every day created new memories, and new cuts and wounds and scratches.

The woman turned and looked at Conrad watching her. For a moment, he didn't register that she had caught him staring at her, and when he did realise, he didn't know what to do. If he looked away, it would imply embarrassment at being caught. But if he continued to stare, it would be worse. Conrad picked up his beer and drank from it deeply. When he put the glass down, he turned his gaze back on the barman, intentionally avoiding looking at the woman. He tried to be as nonchalant as possible, and to pretend that his eyes had rested on her face merely in passing, and now had moved on.

But as Conrad watched the barman, he couldn't help but notice the mirror on the wall behind the bar. The woman was still looking at him. Was she angry that he had stared at her? Surely people stared at her all the time, Conrad thought. He hadn't meant to be disrespectful. The woman drank her wine, slowly, deliberately, and all the while she watched Conrad as he in turn watched her in the mirror.

After a moment or two, the woman stood up. She straitened her skirt and smoothed down her jumper and began to walk towards Conrad. He turned on his stool to face her. She was staring straight at him, walking the short distance over to his bar stool. Conrad felt anxious. What should he do? What would he say? Should he apologise for staring at her?

"Conrad, darling, how are you?" In the end, he was saved by a voice that came from behind him, from the direction of the street door. Conrad knew the voice. It was Heather, his lunch partner. Relief flowed through him and he span on his stool and stood to embrace her.

"I'm so sorry I'm late," Heather said, kissing Conrad. "Traffic's a bitch today."

"Christmas shoppers," Conrad nodded.

"Yes, quite,"

"You look very well," Conrad said, pulling back from her embrace. Heather was in her mid-thirties and looked immaculate: long blond hair, long slim legs, a black trouser suit, and skin with just a hint of ruddy health from the cold air.

"As do you," Heather smiled. "Handsome as ever. And who's this?"

Conrad turned round. The woman with the disfigured face was standing behind him. She was staring at him with a curious expression.

"I don't know," Conrad said, straightening to address the woman. "Can I help you?"

"I wanted to…" the woman began but stopped. Her accent was American. "I'm sorry, I was listening to your conversation. Did I hear your name was Conrad?"

"Yes," Conrad nodded. "Is there something I can do for you?" Standing next to her, so close, and talking to her, her disfigured features didn't seem so daunting.

"I wonder…" The woman stood still, staring at Conrad for a long time, and then at Heather next to him.

"Yes…" Conrad pressed her.

"Do you have the time?" she asked.

"Of course." Conrad rolled up his sleeve and held out his watch so that she could see it. "It's twenty minutes to one."

The woman reached up with her hand and held the watch, staring at its face. She looked back at Conrad and smiled. "Thank you," she said.

"Not at all," Conrad turned back to Heather. "Shall we get a table?"

Conrad called over a waiter and the two of them were directed to a seat by the window and given menus.

"Do you want a drink? How about a bottle of wine?" Conrad asked.

"Who's paying?"

"Me, of course," Conrad shrugged. "You're my PR agent. If you pay, you'll only bill it back to The Cinderella Foundation, with 50% on top."

"Good, shall I choose? White okay with you?"

Conrad nodded and watched the bar again as Heather looked through the wine menu. The woman with the scalded face had returned to her stool. Conrad felt something unusual about their encounter. Her voice seemed familiar to him. From where, he wondered? It was long ago, he was sure of it, but something about that voice had triggered a memory inside him.

Perhaps he had met her before her accident. He couldn't recall meeting anybody with scars like that. But who? When? Conrad reached deep into his sub-conscious, trying to drag the recollection to the surface. Who was she? The edge of the memory lay just beyond him, but he was sure he'd met her before.

"You know that woman at the bar?" Conrad said.

"With the disfigured face?"

"I feel like I've met her before."

"I think you'd remember with a face like that."

"No… there was something about her voice. I think I may have met her before she looked like that. Before her accident…"

"Why don't you go and ask her?"

"Yes," Conrad nodded slowly, "maybe I will."

For more information about this book, or the author, visit:

www.onceuponatimepiece.com

Acknowledgements:

With special thanks to my agent, Diane Banks, for her advice; to everyone at Bo Tree Books; to Samantha Dorri for designing the cover; and to my circle of critics, including Ginny Wood, James MacKinnon, Tom Leander, and Annabel Moore.

Made in the USA
Charleston, SC
20 January 2014